Dedicated to the passionate givers and grateful receivers of love in action.

Chapter One

I wanted some attention, so I hooked up with the 'ho clique'. I thought I could handle it. But I grossly miscalculated the costs.

As I face the consequences, I'm hopeful brighter days lie ahead.

Here is my story.

One day my daddy came home and loved my mama with harsh words and clinched fists. That night we left to make a home in South Park Village, Houston, Texas.

As mama searched for a parking space, I caught a glimpse of our Savior leaning over the balcony smoking a cigarette. Carefree was her first, middle and last name. We called her Aunt Sis, or Auntie for short.

"Hey!" she yelled wildly waving her arms like we hadn't seen her before now. Her strong, throaty voice caught a group of passing teenage boys off guard.

"Damn, she loud."

Mama lightly tooted the horn. "Tre, grab your things. Ned, wake up, boo."

Auntie came downstairs dangling the cigarette between

her lips.

"Hey, lil' mama." I rushed toward her and fell in her arms. Finally, a secure place.

"Hey, man." Auntie reached for Ned's chin and kissed his forehead while I continued to cling to her for dear life.

"Mmm," he mumbled, rubbing away just enough sleep to see his way clear to the stairs.

"Hey," mama said.

Auntie spoke softly. "You all right?"

"I am now." They embraced briefly. Melodrama wasn't their style.

After we carried our luggage upstairs, I joined Ned in Auntie's spare room. Mama placed an ice pack on my forehead.

"Go to sleep." Her swollen, busted lips hindered the usual flawless annunciation of her words.

"But I'm not sleepy, mama."

"You will be. Just close your eyes and lay down."

"Please let me stay up and take care of you, mama. I don't want you hurt any more."

"Shhh...I'm okay. We're okay now. Don't worry about anything." I studied her eyes for reassurance, trying to look past the puffy, black and blue areas surrounding both of them.

"Can you see your way to the door? If not, I can help." The red slits between her eyelashes that use to be big, brown, clear eyes couldn't have offered enough space for her to see.

Exasperated, she placed a finger in front of her mouth. " 'night, Tre." She kissed Ned and me and left the room, closing the door behind her.

I sat in bed debating whether to disobey mama and go to the hallway where I could hear better. My heart finally settled when Auntie laughed and mama joined in. Their giggles were a lullaby to me. Only then was I sure she was okay.

We stayed with Aunt Sis' for about two weeks before moving into Foxwood, a neighboring complex.

On the first day in our new home, I stood under the breezeway looking out wondering what circumstances led my new neighbors to South Park before me. Hundreds of kids and women. Three men.

No invitation came from the girls to play jacks or hopscotch. The boys on bikes ignored me, too. So, I hung out alone praying for the day when the kids in the square would enjoy the pleasure of my company.

The Village could hardly be described as "project living". I mean, we had it a heck of a lot better than James, Florida, JJ, Thelma and Michael. We took cover from the blistering Texas heat under medium-sized elm trees. We swung and seesawed in the complex's park. Swimming pools accommodated the least advanced to the most advanced swim skills. Lighted tennis courts provided us a smooth surface for skating. Each home, I think, served three meals a day. All the kids wore decent clothes and shoes. And for this we thank our mothers, women who effectively handled the affairs of our households despite the absence of men.

Each of the twelve sections in Foxwood formed a square. The enclosed sections created a play area for everyone in that square.

9

Rhone/Premature Pleasures

It was hard to pass through without being noticed. I would eventually grow to hate all of the eyewitnesses.

Chapter Two

"Quit hogging the ball, girl. Dang. You always take too long to throw it back," Lisa chided.

She and Ned were my only two playmates. Of the two, she resented me the most. I acted like a girl. She hated that.

"Yea, Tre. Keep the game going," Ned added. He never challenged her on anything.

At their request, and with all my might, I hurled the ball back towards Lisa. She ran in towards where she thought it would fall and still missed the catch.

"Ugh!" Lisa grunted, rolling her eyes up. Ned put his head down.

"Trekela, why don't you go play with somebody else," Lisa ordered.

That's fine with me. I preferred watching TV to playing Lisa's rough and tumble games anyway. The preparations to fulfill her dreams of being a linebacker or quarterback were brutal on my body.

Heading back towards the square, I bumped into my next door neighbors, Mr. and Mrs. Wilson with their two kids Kayla and lil' Mike.

"Careful!" Mr. Wilson shouted as I turned around in time to miss running into his front. Always dressed business-like, he was one of the three men in the square.

"Sorry," I said.

Lil' Mike favored Mr. Wilson, while Kayla looked like him around the eyes, but had her mama's pooched mouth.

"Hi Trekela! How's your mother?" she asked, sounding like Mrs. Howell from Gilligan's Island.

"She's okay."

"Tell her 'hello' for me, darling."

I walked in the house. "Hey mama."

Staring intently at the television, she ignored me. Reaching for the box of tissues behind her head situated on the end table, she accidentally knocked over her glass of wine.

"Damn!" She turned the glass back up in its upright position.

"I'll get a towel. You want me to pour some more wine for you?"

"No no, Tre. Thanks anyway." She smiled faintly and focused back on her program.

Before the spill caused the wooden table to buckle, I sopped it, trying not to smudge the beveled-glass top. The purple wine looked a lot like grape juice. I wondered if it tasted the same. There was enough wine still in the glass to see for myself.

Just as I lifted it to conduct my own taste test, without warning mama sat up from her lounging position on the sofa, screaming to the top of her lungs. I jumped up and dropped the glass, afraid of what she'd do to me for drinking alcohol.

"I'm sorry, mama."

"Burn him up! Burn his ass up!" She wildly encouraged a black-eyed Farrah Fawcett to pour gasoline on the bed where her adoring husband lay totally at peace.

"We'll return in a moment to 'The Burning Bed' after these messages," the TV announcer said before cutting to a commercial.

Mama rushed past me into the bathroom. I fell on my hands and knees to scrub the brown shag carpet. From the living room, I could hear her crying. After placing the wet towel in the dirty clothes hamper in my bedroom, I went to the bathroom and tapped lightly. "Mama, I'm sitting right outside the door if you need me, okay?"

More time passed, yet I still had no friends. Ned seemed in great company with Lisa. The more I got to know her though, the less I liked her. She always had to have her way. Whatever games we played, she picked. The toys we played with required her blessing. I now understood why the other kids hated her. Since she was bigger than Ned and me, and carried herself like a boy, we didn't want trouble. I mean, we were still the new kids in the square.

But that got old.

One day while sitting on Lisa's steps shifting my focus back and forth between Lisa and Ned to my left and the kickball game in the center of the square in front of me, I noticed Lisa's behavior changed for the worse.

"Ned, I told you to kick it straight," she fussed as she got down on her chest to reach for the ball under the car.

"I can't get it. My arm's too short."

And belly too thick.

"Quit standing there looking stupid. Come get this ball. Dang, it's your fault," Lisa ordered.

Ned obeyed.

"Crawl underneath, stupid. You're shorter than me. I hope you do better next time. 'Cause if you don't, you'll be right back in this position." She shouted her commands at Ned, bending forward to direct instead of kneeling down to assist.

From where I sat, I strained to hear if Ned defended himself. It didn't matter. I refused to sit by any longer letting her talk crazy to my little brother. I knew Lisa was mean, but could she top the drama I'd bring?

Where is my cake knife?

"Lisa!" I yelled.

From the corner of my eye I saw the pitcher hold the kickball, temporarily halting the game.

"Hold up, y'all," he loudly whispered.

"What? Why you screaming my name like you losing yo' mind, girl?"

"Look, cow, I don't appreciate you messin' with my little brother!" I stood defiantly on her steps daring her to make the next move.

"Who you callin' a cow?" She challenged my unspoken dare with quick steps toward me.

"I'm callin' you a cow, you fat, yella' heifah!" I screamed walking toward her, too. In order for me to save face, I had to at least give the appearance that I was the craziest.

"Uh-oh." The crowd murmured as they followed and eventually surrounded us.

We stood face to face, shouting and cussing each other out. Some of the teenagers held our arms behind our backs so we couldn't get to each other before time. They wanted drama, intense and satisfying. There was no telling when the next '*tete a tete*' would happen. So this had to last as long as possible.

"Hold up, y'all. Let's go 'round the corner," one of the older kids suggested.

"Yea, 'cuz we don't want nobody's mama tryin' to stop this," said another one as she held out her hand for her friend to give her five.

Everybody was pumped. They lead us around the corner, on the other side of the washateria. I'm finally getting some attention. And I wanted to make sure to give them their monies' worth. This could be my ticket in finally.

Once in position, they pulled two leaves off the bushes by the washateria. They placed one on my shoulder and one on Lisa's.

"Okay, whichever one a' y'all is the baddest, knock the leaf off the other's shoulder."

Before she could finish giving the instructions, I knocked the leaf off Lisa's shoulder and went straight into a "windmill" all over her. Madness enveloped us. Because I was so out of control, I couldn't see a thing. Occasionally I felt my fist hit firm flesh. Her body was like a microphone, sounding off with each punch landed. When my licks came across more air than body, I looked up to check my position only to see people rolling on the ground holding their stomachs laughing as Lisa sprinted home in tears.

15

At first, I felt sorry for her and ashamed of what I'd done. But that was short lived, especially after I realized there were hands all over me, patting me on the back, trying to give me high five and so on.

"Trekela, you can fight girl!"

"I bet that bitch won't bother you no mo'."

How'd they know my name?

"Trekela, where you from?"

"What grade you in?"

"You know how to play jacks?"

The questions came faster than I was able to respond. So I said nothing, just continued to huff and puff, relishing in the moment.

Eventually, the crowd broke. Surprisingly, the older girls stayed around. Keisha and Erika were the ringleaders.

"Come on, Trekela. Let's go sit on yo' steps," Keisha said.

"Wait a minute." Erika stood in front of me straightening my clothes and stroking my hair back into place. "There you go. We don't want any evidence of your wild side to show through," she smirked.

We sat outside and talked for what seemed like hours. In that one conversation though, I got the skinny on everybody. Talking to them made me see how nothing in this complex is a secret. Eventually, it all comes out.

"Ooh, it's hot as hell out here. Trekela, can we come in yo' house?"

I couldn't believe they wanted to come and hang out with me.

"Hold on. Let me ask my mama." I ran in the house all excited. I couldn't tell her about the fight though. She didn't approve of fighting, even in self- defense. But that policy wouldn't work in the Village.

I knocked on her bedroom door and walked in. "Mama, can my friends come inside to play some of my games?"

"Unh-unh, Tre. Y'all stay outside. I don't feel like all that noise." She pulled the covers over her head.

"Well, can I go to their house then?" I asked desperately searching for middle ground. Now that some of the older girls accepted me, I needed to find a way to stay down.

"No. You don't know those people," she said, not bothering to lift her head from underneath the covers to see in my face how important this was to me.

"Mama, please?" I begged, jumping up and down in the doorway of her room, almost in tears.

"Tre, I said 'no'. Now go sit down somewhere."

I went back outside embarrassed.

"Y'all I can't have company right now. My mama don't feel good."

"Damn. Well, you wanna come to our house?" Keisha offered.

"No, I can't do that neither."

"Yo' mama mean. But that's cool. We'll see you later." They all walked away. I couldn't tell if they felt sorry for me because of mama or because they couldn't spend more time with me. Either way, things were looking up. I was finally in.

Chapter Three

Keisha and Erika proclaimed themselves "queens" of Foxwood. While Keisha lived one section over from me, she always hung out in my square. Erika lived in a whole other complex. I wondered why she stayed with Keisha on and off at times. Looking at them you couldn't tell they were cousins. Keisha, with skin the color of midnight, reminded me of the African dancers that perform every year at Palm Center. Chocolate, graceful and curvaceous. Erika, on the other hand, reminded me of a tomboy, slightly on the thick side. Despite her blotchy light skin and glossy cat-eyes, she was still easy to look at. Everything they did, I wanted to do. Everywhere they went I wanted to go. We mostly hung out in my square, doing each other's hair, listening to Love 94.1 FM and talking. I learned so much from them, mostly about boys.

Both of them had boyfriends they talked about all the time. Shedrick and Milton. Shedrick lived in the front part of our complex. Him and Keisha had been going together since school started. Erika's man Milton lived in Crestmont. I liked him the best. He was cool with me, always treating me like I was part of the crew.

Whenever Keisha or Erika put on lipgloss, that meant Shed or Milton would be in the square some time that day. Watching them walk up was an event by itself. As soon as they knew we noticed them, they'd break into their pop-locking routine, throwing the wave back and forth to each other so they each had a moment in the spotlight. When the routine got old and the spotlight dim, they'd laugh and give each other five, trying to play off their little act.

"Look at them. Always showing out," said Keisha.

"Unh-huh. But you know them niggas can dance!" Erika said turning to Keisha and me with both her hands out. We slapped them in agreement.

"Wait y'all, here they come. Act like you don't see 'em." We all stared into space, looking around like nothing was happening.

"Oh so you gon' act like you don't see a nigga," Shedrick asked with his arms extended. "Keisha, brang yo' fine ass over here and give me some sugar."

At first she looked at him like he was crazy. Who did he think he was talking to her like that? *Make his behind come to you, Keisha*, I thought. Before my thought was complete, she was in his arms, tongue kissing like nobody's business. Milton, Erika and me looked on wondering how long they were gonna act like we weren't there. Milton took Keisha's seat on the steps, kissing Erika on the cheek, then reaching out to give me five.

"What's up, cuz?"

"What's up, Milton," I shot back cool posed, trying to play down my giddiness.

"What's up with you, lil' mama? Over here actin' all quiet and stuff. You ain't happy to see a brotha?"

20

He called it right. She was acting. When he's not around that's all she talks about. Now that he's in her face, she's playing that role. Whatever.

Keisha and Shed finally came up for air from that sloppy looking kiss he planted. Keisha wiped the smudged lipgloss from around her chin and up under her nose.

"What's up, Shed," I said trying to sound cool and see if on this visit I had grown on him, too.

"Hmmm? Oh yea, what's up lil' bit," he offered like he didn't want to be rude, but still didn't wanna speak. Punk.

We sat on the steps for a while talking to each other. Well, Keisha, Erika and me talked to each other, while Shed and Milton clowned amongst themselves. What was the purpose of us sitting together if we didn't share the same conversation? From the looks of things, I was the only one concerned. Shed and Milton were cracking up over something. Keisha and Erika ignored them.

"Say, why don't we walk to the store? A nigga' is thirstier than a mug, man."

Finally something smart from Shed's mouth. I was tired of sitting on the steps anyway. My butt hurt.

We walked to Sunny's. Shed walked with his arm around Keisha's neck and his mouth in her ear the whole time, probably talking nasty. Erika and Milton walked real close to each other, but didn't touch. I felt like an outsider since I didn't have a man. Come to think of it, did they even ask me to tag along with them on their date? Dang.

When we got to the store, I realized I didn't have any money. Keisha and Erika were covered. But who'd cover me?

Oh well. I hung out in the front of the store by the cashier until they were ready to go. The cashier looked familiar. I wanted to get a closer look, but I could see through the big, round security mirror by the door that he was staring at me. Apparently he thought he knew me, too.

"Want anything, Trekela?" Milton startled me from behind.

"That's okay. I don't want anything," I lied.

"Alright nah." He winked at me then walked off.

Erika was so lucky. I wanted a boyfriend like Milton. Tall, pecan-brown colored-skinned, with thick, curly hair crowning the top of his head, he was what Auntie called "easy on the eyes". He walked so tall and strong, like nothing could take him. Above everything else though, he was just so nice, a real gentleman.

As we walked back, they discussed their plans for the evening.

"Say, there's a party at SPN tonight. KJ from Love 94 is deejaying. You know we gots to be there."

Leave it to Shed to plan something I couldn't go to. He probably did it on purpose. Didn't seem to bother anyone else though. They lit up when they found out KJ would be there.

"Ooh, Erika, let me wear yo' black jeans with the matching tank."

"Nope! I ain't even wore 'em yet."

"Come on, Erika. Do me this one solid," Keisha begged.

After further negotiations, Erika consented. Keisha couldn't contain her excitement. She danced around doing booty movements.

22

"You so fast, Keisha," Erika said, shaking her head. "What am I gonna do with you?"

"It's getting late. We need to go get our stuff together. We'll meet y'all at Keisha's place by 8:00 PM," Shed said. "Y'all better be ready on time, too."

"Unh-unh. Wait a minute. Hell no, you can't come to my house. My mama'll be there," Keisha said remembering she wasn't as grown as she thought. "We'll meet y'all at the front section. Then we'll walk over to SPN together."

Shed sucked his teeth and looked at her, suddenly remembering the seven-year age difference between them. "Damn. All right. We'll see y'all at eight. You betta' be there on time, too. I don't wanna have to kick yo' ass." With that, he turned on his heels, threw his hand in the air dismissing everybody. "Let's roll, Milt." The two of them disappeared with less buffoonery than earlier. It didn't matter. The brothers still had style.

"Why you let him talk to you like that," I overheard Erika ask Keisha as they walked off to prepare for their evening.

"Shut up, Erika."

"Bye y'all," I yelled. They obviously forgot I was standing there. Neither of them said anything back. I could see they were arguing. Later on they'll kiss and makeup. I know them. I went back in the house, dreaming of the day I'd be old enough to go out. It wouldn't come soon enough.

I turned the TV on. "What's Happening" was almost over. Handsome, yet slightly on the goofy side, Dwayne was my ideal man. I fantasized about never feeling threatened with him as my boyfriend. I couldn't picture him ever hurting a woman.

After "What's Happening" went off, some white TV show came on. I don't know why the studio audience laughed so hard. Nothing they said or did was that funny. I turned the TV off and went to the kitchen where mama cooked dinner. The frown on her face indicated her head still hurt. Or, maybe she missed daddy.

My world unravels as I watch from under the small opening outside the kitchen. Daddy stumbles into the house, walks into the kitchen and whispers something to Mama as she stands at the stove heating grease to fry chicken. I'm glad to see him acting like he loves her.

"Leave me alone, Sylvester," mama said.

That's a strange response. My signal goes up. Then he approaches her again, whispering in her ear. This time she screams out through tears, "LEAVE ME ALONE!"

That which before quietly brewed underneath finally surfaced.

"Mama!" I scream.

Daddy punches her in the stomach. She falls forward. My world fell apart. He grabs her by the hair and pulls her into their bedroom with mama screaming and crying out in pain, but not fighting back. He locks the door behind him so I can't follow them. Mama continues screaming, at times getting louder.

What is he doing to her? And I can't help her. I kick the door, screaming and crying until my stomach started hurting.

"Mama... please...daddy... no..." I cry over and over. I am helpless.

I run to my room to get Ned. He sleeps carefree on the top bunk, unmoved by the drama going on between mama and daddy.

I go back to their door, but can't hear anything. I panic.

"Daddy, please let me come in!!#", I scream. The door opens. His clothes are all messed up, self-inflicted no doubt. He is sweating up a storm and never looks at me. I can tell the pitbull rage hasn't left. I lunge in front of him trying to get to the bathroom to check on mama. She sobs quietly, sitting on the edge of the tub, her face buried in her hands.

"Ma-ma?" I approach her slowly, my vision blurred from the tears, my words broken by hiccups. As she lifts her head, I hardly recognize her. Black and blue bruises, traces of blood are all over her face.

"Ma-ma, your face…" I touch her. She pulls me close to her and puts her finger over my mouth. Tears still stream, but we try to keep it to a minimum. We don't want to upset the demon now possessing the man I call 'daddy' and mama call's 'sweetie' anymore than he already is. Softly sobbing but more at ease now that I know mama is okay, I think about how different this scene could be right now if mama had allowed that hot chicken grease to be her defense.

"Shut up all that goddamn crying, both of you!" Daddy yells. But I can't help it. Mama tries to console me, but I only cry harder. In a fit of rage, daddy jumps up, grabs me by the arm as mama looks on in horror. Effortlessly, he tosses me into the wall in the hallway and re-locks the door.

"Please God…please God…please God…" I plead as I

camp outside their door, waiting on Him to answer. Eventually, daddy walks out the bedroom, then out the apartment and slams the door. I rush to mama's side to console her.

"Mama, are you okay? Mama, let's leave before he comes back. Let's just go." She looks in my eyes, tears streaming. As she strokes my hair, she lifts her head and closes her eyes for a few seconds. She looks back in my eyes and smiles.

"Mama, you need some help?"

"No," she said, not looking up.

"Is everything okay?"

"Yea," she said dryly, again, not facing me.

It seemed like forever since we left him. I wondered what was he doing right now? Did he know where we were? If so, why didn't he call?

Ned came in breathing hard, sweat pouring down his face. He'd just finished racing. Knowing him, he came in last place. But that never stopped him from trying. He went straight to the kitchen.

"Hey mommie," he smiled.

"Hey man," mama smiled back looking down at him. She hadn't seen him all day. "You hungry?"

"Yes, ma'am," he said, rubbing his stomach. Mama was amused by his gesture. Watching them interact made me wish I had someone who thought I was special, too. I missed Sis. Lightner. She was the only person I could think of who made me feel treasured. When I entered a room she'd lean over to whoever was close and say 'See there, now here comes *my* baby!'

Sis. Lightner was an old lady who picked me up for Sunday School and church every Sunday when we lived with my daddy. She wore a white nurse uniform with the matching hat. I don't know how she knew mama. She didn't live in our complex and she looked too old to work. Yet each Sunday, she'd come get me. Before walking into church, she'd give me a peppermint candy.

"Don't eat ya candy in church, baby, okay? You look so beautiful this morning. You're God's special angel, you know that?" she said to me each Sunday. And I believed her. There was something about the way she looked at me. She had something very precious. I wanted that *something* for myself. I wanted that for my family.

Chapter Four

Erika went back home. No telling when I'd see her again. But she'd be back. So, Keisha and I started hanging out. I loved Keisha so much. I wished I could be just like her. As we walked home from the store one time, we passed by Shed's apartment in front of the tennis court.

"Hold up, Trekela. Let's stand here for a minute. I wanna see if Shed is gon' come outside or not." We squatted behind some tall shrubbery, looking crazy. The silence didn't help. We were so obvious.

"What do you like about Shed?" I asked, wanting to know how someone as beautiful as Keisha could settle for someone as trifling as Shed. He didn't seem anywhere near her level. Looking at them you couldn't tell they'd have anything in common, except their environment. Maybe that was enough.

"He's sooo fine. Plus, he kisses real good. He's the one who taught me how to kiss. The boys at my junior high school are so immature. Their asses are still into Matchbox cars. No ma'am. I need a real man. Everybody wants Shed. But he only wants me."

29

I'd hoped for a more meaningful answer. You know, something that would explain why we're camped outside this nigga's apartment hiding in the bushes. I still wasn't over him threatening to kick her ass for something as simple as being late to their meeting spot. Even if she was late, she was worth the wait. But maybe he didn't think so. Or worse, she didn't.

Shed built quite a reputation for himself with the ladies. Every baseball cap he owned was branded with the playboy symbol. I never saw him with anyone other than Keisha. But there were lengthy periods when we didn't know where he was. Take for instance, right now. Keisha was trying to play cool about it. I could tell she was bothered, no hiding that. Moments like this reminded me Keisha was still a little girl herself, trying desperately to play like she was grown. Right now, she was failing with a capital "F".

"Trekela, I wanna tell you somethin' because you're like my best friend now." *Really*?! I went crazy with excitement on the inside, but played it cool.

"Sure, Keisha. What's up?"

"Chile, guess what Shed asked me?" she said with her mouth pursed and twisted. Whatever it was, she wasn't having it.

"That fool had the nerve to ask me when was I gon' 'prove' my love to him. And you know what that means."

Unh-huh. She was about to be grown for real.

"What should I do?"

"The way you was looking just a second ago, I thought your decision was made," I said attempting to sound mature. I gave my effort an "A".

"I don't wanna lose him. I've never done it before, not all the way. I mean, I've let niggas play with my titties and grind on me. But you can't get pregnant from that."

This conversation was getting deep, too deep for me. My knees hurt from squatting in the bushes. I took a seat on the dirt. Hopefully, it'll wash off my clothes. Being here with Keisha gave me another view of relationships. At this moment, they didn't seem worth all the trouble. Most of the time everything appeared cool. I wonder how her mama feels about...never mind. I don't even need to take that thought any further. Hollywood lied to us everyday on TV with images of mothers and daughters being able to talk openly. Humph.

Keisha joined me on the ground.

I knew Shed wasn't worthy to receive what Keisha could only give once in her life. Keisha was smart enough to see through him. Why was this decision so difficult for her? I hated being the one to tell her the right thing to do.

"In my opinion," I said, "you should do it."

Far be it from me to do what I hate.

"Really?" Keisha asked, holding on to every word that came from my lips.

"Unh-huh. I would," I lied.

She let out a sigh of relief. We looked at each other, looked up at our immediate surroundings and fell out laughing. Enough of this mess. We got up from the dirt, dusted our shorts off, and walked back to the square chatting about nothing. As we cut through the parking lot, a car came up slowly alongside us, blasting music. We tried to play it off, but whoever this was wanted us to notice. The car pulled up enough for us to sneak a peek through the passenger window. We looked inside on the sly. It was the cashier from Sunny's, the corner store. I knew I recognized him. He lives in the back section of the complex. He exchanged *knowing* glances with Keisha. There was history between them.

But I didn't wanna know it.

Chapter Five

It didn't take long for everyone to notice how tight Keisha and I had gotten. Our nosy neighbor, Ms. Pat, would always watch us as we walked through the square.

"Look at her lil' nasty ass swishing through here like she somebody," she'd say loud enough for us to hear her as she sat self-righteous upstairs peering out of bloodshot red eyes, holding a tall, brown paper bag known simply as her 'companion'.

Keisha didn't care. As long as she got attention, she was cool. Ms. Pat's comments bothered me though. I couldn't tell if she was talking about me, too.

Since doing it with Shed, Keisha did seem to act and dress a little different. No mistaking she thought she was the stuff now. Her shorts got shorter, her pants got tighter and every top managed to find a way to show off her stomach, whether it was made that way or not. He'd opened a whole new world for her. Still didn't bring him around anymore than usual. But now Keisha had other brothas flocking around her like birds feeding on breadcrumbs thrown to them by Galveston Island tourists…suddenly.

Forget Shed. Who needs him?

I envied Keisha so much. The more time I spent with her, the more I wanted to be like her. I wished I could be bold and have an "I don't care what you think" attitude. Nothing anyone said phased her. She'd just go on her merry way.

Erika's younger brother Curtis would come over to hang out in our complex from time to time. He was so cute. Curtis was about my age, light brown skin with tight curly hair and cat eyes like Erika. I loved to watch him come through the square and pop "wheelies" on his bike.

One day Keisha and I played jacks on my porch. It was my turn. But when I bounced the ball my eyes caught Curtis riding through the square on the back wheel, the front wheel suspended in the air. Now that was a good wheelie. The ball bounced on top of one of the jacks and messed up the formation.

"Damn, Trekela, pay attention," Keisha said.

Here's my chance to finally play big girl where it really counted.

"How old is Curtis?"

"Ten years old. Why?" Keisha asked, obviously missing my hint.

"He sure is cute."

"Oooh, you like Curtis?" Keisha asked, amused and at full attention.

"Unh-huh. You don't think he's cute?"

"Girl, that's my cousin! I ain't lookin' at him like that. He's too young for you anyway."

Obviously my being tall for my age had her confused with how old I really was.

"How's he too young for me? We're the same age."

"You only 10?" Keisha looked at me with a confused expression. That's only two years younger than she is. Why is she tripping?

"Yea. So what?"

"Damn, Trekela," she laughed. "I thought you were with me. Look at you. Yo' titties bigger than mine."

Like her chest size was hard to beat.

"If I was with you, wouldn't I also be at Albert Thomas?"

"I figured you were bused out to Pershing or Welch or one of the other white schools. I mean, look how you talk."

Something told me I should be offended by that comment.

"Why yo' mama make you go to school out there with those white folks anyway?"

"I don't know. I wanted to go to school with the kids around here. But she didn't ask my opinion. Besides, there are other black kids at my school."

"What side of town are they *bused* from? I know they don't live over there," she added sarcastically.

Now that she mentioned it, every black child at my school caught the bus to school. The white kids were the only ones who rode bikes to class and served as cross guards.

"I guess mama thought we'd get a better education through the magnet schools."

"Ain't nothin' wrong wit' the schools over here. Didn't they make you fill out a application and stuff?"

"I don't know. Mama did everything. It couldn't have been too difficult. She did it."

"Well, my mama thought about it. But them white folks wanted her to jump through too many hoops. So she said, fuck em'."

Now that she knew how old I was, I hoped this wouldn't affect our friendship. Everything was suddenly clear to her now. Whenever she'd talk about dressing out for gym, or share what happened in first, second and third period, or getting pops for chewing gum, I didn't have a clue what she was talking about. In elementary school, our school clothes *were* our gym clothes. We sat in the same class all day taught by one teacher. Anybody caught chewing gum had to go to the conduct board, and move their name down. Rather than let on I didn't have a clue what she was talking about, I'd just shake my head, laugh on cue and throw in an occasional "me, too" or "I can't stand when that happens".

We talked some more about school and how shocked she was, but no more about Curtis.

A few weeks later, while hanging outside on the steps watching a practice kickball game, Curtis rode up on his bike. He'd been riding through doing his usual bike tricks. I pretended not to notice him. My eyes were glued to the practice game. But my mind was fixed on him.

Please God let him stop.

Out the corner of my eye I saw him hop off his bike, and walk towards the stairs where I sat. *Hey...*

"Boo!" he yelled.

"Ahhh!" I faked. "Curtis, you scared me," I rolled my eyes and turned my head away from him and back towards the game so he wouldn't see the grin on my face.

He put his bike down, came on the stairs and sat two steps up from me to watch the game, too. The boys looked good. Their kicks packed power. Never mind they spent more time on the roof getting the ball down than they did on the "field". They just might beat Orleans. I hope they do. Orleans think they're the best at everything.

"Man, them niggas are sorry. Orleans gon' kill them," Curtis said after watching them for a minute.

"I know, huh?" Team loyalty was not my immediate goal. "You ought to go out there and show 'em how to do it."

We sat in silence watching the boys practice. The cheerleaders also practiced their routines. The cheerleaders, or Foxes at Foxwood, knew how to turn heads. They were good dancers, especially Chanel. Chanel was probably the most naturally beautiful girl in our complex. Carmeled-colored skin, perfectly symmetrical almond-shaped light brown eyes accentuated by long eyelashes and perfectly straight teeth. On top of that, she smiled all the time. It was hard for me to feel good about myself in her presence. Still doesn't change the fact that they needed to learn some new cheers. I was sick of "Rock Steady".

As I sat with Curt, I realized they posed a little more competition than what I wanted. How could I keep his interest?

"What grade are you in, Curt?" I tried to think of something better to say. Nothing came. Hopefully this was enough to get him to at least help me fan the flames of our *love*.

"Fifth grade. What grade are y...ah damn! Those brothas need some help," he said disgusted by the fumble or foul or strikeout, whatever happened on the field. "I'll catch ya later."

There went the love of my life. I wondered could he kiss. Do I even know the difference between a good kiss and a bad one? Time would tell.

I hated to see him leave. That was my first time alone with him. Lately I fantasized about our love affair. With my eyes closed, I imagined him pulling me close.

"Trekela, you are so beautiful. I've never met a girl like you," he'd say as he brushed my bangs from my forehead, followed by a long, hot tongue kiss.

"I'll never let you go, Tre."

"Curt, let's stay together for always and forever."

"Tre - what the hell are you doing?" I opened my eyes and closed my mouth and legs as mama stood in front of me with her hands on her hips and the trademark frown. "What the hell did I just see you doing?"

"Nothing," I said embarrassed, hoping she hadn't seen me act out what I'd been thinking.

"Bring your fast ass in this house," she yelled pointing towards our door. One hand rested on her hip, while her frown carved deep wrinkles in her forehead showing how pissed off she was. All activity in the square stopped. No cheers, no kickball. Everyone stood quietly, watching to see what would happen next. They loved drama.

Lord, please don't let her hit me outside in front of all these people.

I got up from the stairs, not wanting to look at anybody directly. As I passed mama, I purposely stayed out of arm's reach, just in case my prayer came up short.

"What do you think you were doing out there? Where'd you learn that from?"

I didn't answer.

Once we closed the door, all at once I heard a burst of laughter. What's so funny? And why'd it have to happen after I went inside?

I parked myself in front of the television careful to stay out of mama's way. Still angry, she went back to her room cussing and fussing. She slammed the bedroom door behind her.

I'll never show my face in the square again.

Chapter Six

My only view to the world outside of #1258-D was through the curtains. From time to time I'd peek out and see Curt ride through the square. I haven't seen Keisha in a while. So much for being best friends. She was out there now. I really missed her though. It'd been a while since we had girl talk. Plus, I wanted to hear the latest on Shed, even though there probably wasn't much to tell. The last time I saw him, he was cat-calling outside Sunny's. I hoped Keisha knew what kind of man he was. My grandmama said some men are a waste of "mattah". Although unsure of what "mattah" was, I'm pretty certain she meant Shed. I also wanted to know the low-down on Curt. Keisha could advise me. I refused to believe the only reason he stopped by was to watch the guys practice.

He had to like me, too. What other explanation was there for his hanging out in my square? Boys at his age drove me nuts. They know they like you, but they'd rather play games.   Maybe I'd help him out a little bit.

If my bike wasn't on flat, I'd ride through the hills with him and, you know, get some real action. The hills were a perfect spot to get whatever you wanted.

I wanted Curt.

One day, Chanel rode through the square on her pink frame bike with the white trunk seat, and pink and white flowing streamers dangling from the handlebars. The bike, like Chanel, made me sick. It was perfect just like her. And she was free to roam the sidewalks throughout the complex with no shame, unlike me who was trapped in the house like an Iranian hostage.

As I sat there thinking of other reasons why I hated Chanel, Curt rode through. He'd been passing my house all afternoon. I brushed my hair up around the sides and back and tightened my ponytail at the crown of my head. Searching frantically for mama's lipgloss but coming up empty, I settled on Vaseline.

Before leaving the house, I examined myself one last time.

Honk, honk, honk.

I peeked out the window to see Chanel signal Curt to let her pass. But he kept coming. One of them needed to decide quick to get off the sidewalk before they ran into each other. Just in the knick of time Curt jumped his bike on to the grass, but not before reaching out to grab Chanel's titties.

She giggled. "Stop, Curt, with your nasty self."

Curt's bony behind slowed down, turned his bike around and pursued Chanel. Worse still, she didn't try very hard to get away from him. Ho'.

Weeks sauntered by leisurely during my house arrest. Very little held my attention on TV. The more I watched, the more I was convinced the 'live studio audience' was stupid.

Nothing Jack, Crissy and Janet did on "Three's Company" was that funny. The audience *must* get paid.

Mama remained in her bedroom, coming out with a crinkled face only to cook or go to work or fuss.

"I have a headache, Tre. Take that noise outside."

So, to the outside I went and sat on the steps.

No one seemed to notice me at first. They were too into the dodgeball game.

" 'cuse me, Trekela." Ms. Sheila from upstairs walked past me carrying groceries. She's the school secretary over at Frost Elementary. "You okay?"

"Unh-huh."

"Unh-huh?" she asked looking at me for a different answer.

"Yes, ma'am."

"Hey, Pat. Chile, what's goin' on?" Ms. Sheila and Ms. Pat lived next door to each other.

"Honey, tryin' to make it," Ms. Pat responded, sitting in a chair she pulled outside from her dining room table. She used her towel to swat at a wasp. Ms. Sheila unlocked her door and went inside.

The game looked like so much fun. I would join in, but…oh yeah, my legs hurt. Besides, I have more fun watching dodgeball than playing it.

Ouch! Dee Dee got hit in the head. I knew it hurt. But she wouldn't show it. Walking out the dodgeball circle she looked around for a seat until the next game. She looked dead at me sitting by myself and walked the other way. China doll looking, slew-foot walking heifa', carting all that butt around like it's a chore.

"Girl, I am not fat. My butt just big, that's all," she'd say. Whatever.

I'm glad she didn't bring her two-faced self over here. The last time I spent time with her on her porch, she showed her true colors.

"Look at them. They think they cute. You could tell they got different daddies. Why is Stephanie's hair real wavy compared to Vanessa's? I mean, she got good hair, too, but not as good as Stephanie's."

Listening to her go on and on about their private business got old. The way she talked, I thought she couldn't stand them. Until…

"Hey, Van . Hey Steph! Y'all look cute!" she yelled from the porch.

Huh?

I couldn't believe her. Not two seconds earlier she was running them through the mud. She is so fake. Watching this whole scene I wondered what she said about me behind my back.

"Hey," Stephanie said real dry. Vanessa didn't bother speaking. They already knew.

I felt bad getting all their family business from Dee Dee. But I really didn't know them, other than they were one of the three families in the square where the man in the house was married to their mother. I used to wish I had hair like Stephanie. Then I wouldn't have to keep going to the beauty shop for retouches. I'd give anything to not have my scalp burned just to get straight hair.

Although Dee Dee talked too much, she usually told what other people thought. I never understood their family situation. Like, the mom worked everyday, but the stepdad stayed home. Almost everyday he'd put the speaker outside the door, have his partners on the porch playing dominoes, smoking and drinking. Other times, Stephanie couldn't go in the house, even though her stepdad and Vanessa were there, but not her mom.

"Stephanie, where Vanessa at?" a group of kids would surround her and ask.

"She in the house," Stephanie would say not looking up.

"What she doin'?"

Stephanie wouldn't respond verbally. She'd shrugged her shoulders. We knew not to press the issue.

More people lined the sides of the dodgeball game than were actually in the game itself. Early and David showed no mercy to the remaining three in the center. They went after Todd for real. They tried to kill him. I guess it was all good since he laughed and talked trash.

"What's up? Y'all ready to give up?" Todd ducked a shot intended for his head.

Early and David's sly attempts to get him out failed. They decided instead to go after Angie and Wayne, two easier targets. Rather than throwing the ball at each one, David tossed the ball overhead to Early, who caught it faster than Angie or Wayne was able to move. POW! The ball smacked Angie on the side of her face.

"Damn it, Early. That's fucked up! Why'd you have to hit her like that, punk? I wish yo' ass'd hit me like that," Wayne said as he helped Angie up from the ground. Tears glossed over her eyes but didn't fall.

"Man, forget you and her. If she can't roll, she needs to stay her ass out the game," Early said, positioning the ball under his arm, waiting to see if he'd need to put it down and scrap. Early was normally pretty cool. It wasn't like him to cuss a girl. But Wayne embarrassed him. And he couldn't come off as soft in front of his boys.

"Let's finish the game, man. Angie got hit, so she's out," Todd said. He danced around looking agitated.

I hated him. Couldn't he see there was a mini crisis? Wayne and Angie were almost like brother and sister. Wayne's father and Angie's mother went together. They lived in the section up front by the pool and tennis court. Wayne earned major points from me that day for sticking up for Angie.

The argument heightened between Early, Todd, and Wayne. As the sidelined girls tended to Angie, I caught a glimpse of a figure coming in from around the washateria. It was a girl bent over, holding her stomach. No one else saw her. They were too into the "dodgeball brawl". I stood up where I could see she was leaving a trail behind her. From my viewpoint, I couldn't see what it was. She lifted her head slowly. I saw her face. *Oh my God...*

"KEISHA!" I leaped from the stairs. "Please God, please...Keisha, oh God, what happened to you?"

46

By now, all eyes were glued on Keisha, yet no one panicked but me. Everyone else drew back, wide-eyed, covering their mouths, speechless and frightened.

"What happened to Keisha?" they whispered.

Keisha's bloodied and bruised face was more than I could handle. Her ripped halter exposed her right breast. Her shoes were missing. She tried to talk, but I had a difficult time understanding her words.

I examined her face, touching it lightly, then looked down at the trail. Oh my God…it's blood! But the blood on her face wasn't trickling. Where was all the blood coming from? Starting from the cut on her forehead, I worked my eyes down her face to her throat, down to her chest, but nothing was there. My eyes traveled further south and noticed her white shorts were red on the bottom.

That was a weird fashion - two-tone shorts. They didn't even match her green halter. On second look though, her shorts were torn in the crotch, and the red was BLOOD!

I swallowed hard, but said nothing. Here was the red and wet proof that Keisha was out there.

She remained bent over, as blood still marked her tracks while she took baby steps towards her section with my help.

I looked at Keisha all battered and bruised and saw mama.

"Trekela, what's wrong with Keisha?" Dee Dee asked. Ten minutes before she worked overtime ignoring me. Now she sniffed at my behind, dying to get the scoop, looking like she really cared about Keisha. Screw her. Screw all of them.

Now I ignored them.

I helped Keisha walk towards her apartment. I tried desperately to ease her physical pain as much as possible. That was easiest for now. Years would pass before she'd heal emotionally. I didn't want to go there.

As we journeyed slowly to her apartment, I couldn't help thinking if Keisha brought this on herself. She loved attention. When it came to men, anything went. I use to envy her sexual confidence and freedom. Now I've witnessed the flip side of her liberty. I used to admire the attention she got. From where I sat, it seemed harmless.

Once we reached Keisha's section, she couldn't walk up the stairs. She motioned for me to go knock on the door. I ran up the steps skipping two or three at a time to reach the top faster. From the top step I overheard Keisha's mother's voice crystal clear. She was on the phone with the front window open and curtains closed.

"Chile, I don't know where her pissy tail is. She runnin' 'round here somewhere," Ms. Linda said, obviously referring to Keisha. I knocked on the door.

"Shirley, hold on a minute. Who the hell is it?" she yelled, mad about her conversation being interrupted.

"Ms. Linda, it's Trekela. Keisha is..."

"Keisha's ass ain't here. I'll tell her you came by, shit. Bye," she dismissed me, and continued her conversation. "Shirley, I'm back. What was I sayin..."

"Ms. Linda!" I boldly yelled through her screen window.

Before I could say another word, she yanked the front door open, phone glued to her ear with the cord wrapped around her arm, poised to wrap it around my neck.

"Girl, have you lost your godda...ahh, Keisha!" She dropped the phone and rushed past me, her reddish blond hair pulled back in a ponytail exposing an inch of black new growth.

"Keisha, what the hell happened?" Her voice quivered. "What have you done?" Ms. Linda looked over Keisha's face, stroking it slightly, then down at the tear between Keisha's legs. She poked around the area carelessly, ignoring Keisha's cries of discomfort. Afterwards she looked up at Keisha.

Her lips were turned upwards in a snarl. She looked mad enough to kill. In her face, I saw my father.

"When you walk around here lookin' and actin' like a ho', expect to be treated like one."

Keisha sobbed uncontrollably. Without looking at me, "You can go home now," Ms. Linda said in a low voice. "Keisha, bring ya ass upstairs."

I walked off hesitantly, every few seconds looking back to watch Keisha struggle with each step, her right arm clumsily tossed across her mama's neck, her head bowed low, tears streaming from her once beautiful face. The further I got from the stairs, the less I could hear Ms. Linda's brutal comments. Although not yelling, her words still hit like blows to the stomach. But none were as savage as the final audible comment.

"I bet yo' chocolate ass won't sling that twat around everywhere now, will you? You'll settle down now, huh?" They disappeared into the apartment.

Walking back to my square, I felt guilty. Not thirty minutes before I secretly hoped for tragedy to strike someone else so that my spotlight of shame would shift elsewhere. At first, all I thought about was returning to my normal life. I was sick of being alone, of not being able to choose to be with the "in" group. *God, please forgive me for being so selfish.*

"Trekela!" All the kids raced towards me as I turned the corner back into the square.

"What happened to Keisha?"

"Yea, who beat her up?"

Who beat her up? Stupid, thy name is Dee Dee, Early, Dava, Todd and whoever else thought like them.

"I don't know. She wouldn't tell me what happened," I responded, my head hung low, my voice even lower admittedly for dramatic effect. One by one they shared what they believe happened.

"She probably got jumped by some girl for messing with her man."

"I bet she took a shortcut through Crestmont. Keisha know them girls over there can't stand her."

"Unh-unh. I know who did this to her…"

"Who?" echoed through the group.

"Shed!" Everyone voted him the likely culprit. Shed did have a mean streak. In the past, he had threatened to kick her ass for one reason or another many times. Maybe he found out about her and all those other guys, caught her alone, forced

50

her to the trails to punch and kick her all over her body. Punk! His day would come.

I let a few weeks pass before I dared go over to Keisha's apartment again. Afraid of what I'd see, I was two seconds from asking Dee Dee of all people to walk over there with me. She was the only one bold, or nosy enough to go with me. But I didn't want her going back reporting everything. And, if Ms. Linda cussed me out, I didn't want any witnesses. I made my decision. I would go alone.

My stomach tumbled around my insides. Fear paralyzed me. After all, Ms. Linda wasn't the most rational person. If she'd treat her own bloodied, bruised daughter like a three-legged stray mutt, I know she wouldn't show me love. I rehearsed my lines. Walking towards the back of the complex, I was nervous like a pimp in a prayer meeting. Whatever happened to me wouldn't be nearly as bad as what happened to Keisha. Turning the corner, I glanced down and noticed a faded trail of brown spots. Tears welled in my eyes.

"Keisha." I sighed softly. I don't care what anyone says, no one ever does anything to deserve that. No one.

My stomach tightened the closer I drew to the stairs. The last time I climbed these steps, I was anxious to get to the top. Now, I took them one at time, positioning my feet on the part that didn't have dried bloodstains. Midway up I saw the curtains pulled wide open. A good sign. People who had something to hide or who wanted to remain private closed themselves up in their apartments. Open curtains and windows always seemed like a friendly gesture. It's like saying, "Come on in!" I was less afraid then. I'd hoped Keisha was in the living room.

51

I pictured reaching the top step, and Keisha opening the door.

"TREKELA!"

"Keisha!"

We'd embrace and laugh and hug each other.

"Trekela, I've missed you so much. Thanks for being there for me. I don't know what I would have done without you."

"You're my girl. You know I'd do anything for you."

"Mama has made me stick close to the house since the incident."

"At least you're healing well."

"Yea, well, it's taking longer than I'd like. But I'll be beautiful again. Watch me."

"You're still beautiful."

I peaked through the window. My hands cupped my forehead to remove the sun's glare. I blinked repeatedly trying to get my eyes to see what was there. But there was nothing to see. The apartment was empty. I stood there dazed for a minute, jolted back to reality by something wet crawling down my face. Was I sweating that much?

No. I finally released my tears. I allowed them to flow for my friend and my loss.

Chapter Seven

When Mimi and Nae moved to the square, they brought the devil with them. Cute enough to be models, they preferred instead to act like hoes and mini-gangsters.

I met them for the first time coming home from checking the mailbox.

"Trekela!"

"Huh?"

"Come here for a minute," Nae said.

Nae stood on the porch leaning over the rail skillfully sucking a Blowpop. She obviously knew how to get to the bubble gum in the middle without cracking the candy shell. Mimi sat on the top step, legs gapped open, licking the peppermint stick in the center of her pickle. As I approached the stairs, it seemed the pickle and Blowpop got more attention than me. I know I heard her call me over to them.

Halfway up, Nae looked at me. "I heard you been talkin' 'bout us."

"Unh-unh! Who told you that?"

"Don't worry 'bout who told us. We wanna kno' what you said?"

"I haven't said anything to anyone about you. Who's been lying on me?"

My heart pounded against my chest like it was trying to escape. Peeling paint from the stair rail stuck to my sweaty palms. Who would blatantly lie on me? Dee Dee! Her fat butt was the only one messy enough to do something like that. She probably did it so that she could get in good with them.

Should I run home and lock the door while I had a chance, or stay and take the butt whooping they'd give me? Right as I decided to make a break for it I caught them grinning at me. They looked at each other and fell out. Mimi laughed so hard she accidentally dropped her pickle causing them to laugh harder.

Nae walked over to where Mimi laid out and slapped her five. "We jus' messin' wit' you. Girl, ain't nobody said nothin' about you."

If they wanted to get to know me, all they had to do was say so. My heart settled.

"Come on up and talk to us for a while," Nae said.

"Hand me my pickle," Mimi said.

"Ooh, Mimi, you nasty."

"Tell me somethin' I don't know." Turning to me, "I like yo' jumper. That's cute." Mimi referred to my oversized white denim coveralls.

She was right. It was a cute day for me.

"How long you lived over here?"

"Almost two years."

"You like it around here?"

"It's okay. Everybody is pretty cool. I usually stick to myself though."

"Where yo' mama work at?"

"She work downtown for an oil company. She's a secretary."

"I knowed she had a professional job," Nae said turning to Mimi who agreed. "Sometimes when our mama is just getting in from work, we see yo' mama leavin' for work."

"And she be sharp as a tack, too," Mimi offered again referring to clothes.

Yea, I guess mama did dress real nice, especially when comparing it to their mama's blue tunic with her name on a patch.

"Yo' mama must make a lot of money, too. We see all that nice furniture in y'all's house."

"And you always wear cute clothes," Mimi added.

"Well, I don't know if she make all that much money. Look at our raggedy car!"

We all laughed in agreement. The sure sign anybody had money around here was in what they drove. And for all the money we supposedly had, that little red Toyota with the missing grille was all we had to show for it. But at least we had a car, which is more than I could say for them.

"You must favor your daddy." Nae scrutinized my face. "Mimi, look at her eyes. You wear eyeliner?"

55

"No, why?"

"Your eyes are so big. But they pretty though."

"Let me see your hand." I reached out to her. She put hers next to mine. "We the same color."

"Yea, but she way cuter than you," Nae remarked.

"Kiss my ass. I look good, too. Ask yo' man about me!"

"You don't look nothin' like yo' brother. Y'all got the same daddy?"

"Of course we've got the same daddy!"

"You sure?" Mimi couldn't control herself. She fell out. I didn't find her comment funny at all.

"Why you never wear your hair down? You like it up in a ponytail?" Mimi asked.

"If my hair was as thick as yours, I'd wear it down all the time," Nae said.

"It's thick because I need a relaxer."

"Oh."

I listened to them go on and on about nothing. Everything out their mouth had to do with sexing boys and fighting girls.

That's why I was thrown off guard by the question that brought me back into the conversation.

"Trek, answer something for me."

What a cute nickname. I guess that means we're girls now.

"Why come y'all don't go to church 'round here like us? Y'all don't believe in God or something?"

A lot of good going to church was doing these tramps.

56

Not two minutes earlier they plotted to violate at least seven of the Ten Commandments. That comment pissed me off a little. I mean, it wasn't like I robbed or killed people. Still, I hadn't been to church in a long time. Looking at them, I questioned the need to go since I acted more like Christ than these tight shorts wearing, trash talking, "screw anything not nailed down" hoes.

But for some reason, the question pierced me to the heart and made me long for Sis. Lightner.

I use to love for Sister Lightner to pick me up for church. I don't know why. Actually, Sunday services at True Vine Full Gospel Church scared me kinda. All around me were people shouting and getting happy. Some even fell out. Sister Lightner and the other nurses would fan and hold the wailing arms of these people. What made them act like that?

"Thank you, Jesus. Thank you, Lord!," was proclaimed all over the building as the church people caught the Holy Ghost.

It was a crazy scene. Made me wonder how bad I wanted God if He made me act like that in front of people.

Not everyone carried on so. Many of the people sat quietly to themselves, head bowed low, crying softly. A neighbor might put their arms around them and rock gently. I knew something was wrong in their life. Even though I was young, I related to their heartache. I cried for whoever failed them. A shared faith in God both united and sustained us every Sunday morning at 11:00AM. I'd look to the back pew and see mama as one of those quietly hoping.

"Saints, Jesus is the only one who could change your bad situation to good. Make a commitment to try Him this week," the preacher admonished.

Okay, pastor, we'll give Him a shot, I thought. But if He don't act soon, we'll have to change it ourselves.

I tried desperately to find examples of my goodness as a defense. "I believe in God. I say grace over my food before I eat, and I pray each night before I go to sleep. I think I'm good enough."

"Well, baby, good enough ain't gon' do. You need Jesus," Mimi said giving that dirty pickle a break, looking towards Nae as her Amen corner.

"Preach, my sister!" Nae yelled out. She lifted her hands, closed her eyes, bowed her head waving it side to side and jumped around pretending she got the Holy Ghost. "Yes, Lord! Yes, Lord! Halleluuuujah!"

"Aye… Nae you crazy." Mimi enjoyed Nae's little antics. When I looked at her though, I saw the woman in church I tried to not sit next to because you didn't know what she'd do when the Spirit hit her.

I grinned a little at Nae's charades. I also watched the heavens for lightning bolts with her name on it.

Suddenly, the door cracked open. James Cleveland's "No Way Tired" played softly in the background. From the doorframe came the voice of Nae and Mimi's little sister Mary.

"Oooh, Nae, I'ma tell mama you out here playin' with God." Being severely buck toothed, she pronounced every word beginning with a consonant letter like the letter "F" was attached to it. She quickly closed and locked the door.

Nae kicked it and beat her fist against the window.

"I'm gon' kick yo' ass when I get inside. You can't lock me out all day. I *will* get back in, and when I do…," she didn't complete the sentence. She pulled her shorts down from the crotch, then from the back, only intending to show the base of her butt cheeks.

We sat outside until their mama Ms. Ruth walked up.

"Why aren't you inside getting dressed for bible study and prayer meeting?"

"Mary locked us out, mama."

"I know when I get upstairs that house betta' be clean."

"Mama, we been locked out! Mary wouldn't let us come in to do our work, huh Trekela?"

Leave me outta this.

"Huh, Trekela?" Nae insisted.

"Unh-huh," I murmured.

"Unh-huh. Get in the house. And you," pointing to me, "go home."

After seeing her up close, I decided Nae and Mimi must favor their daddy. She wouldn't be too bad looking if Jesus gave her a reason to smile. He could also throw in a tube of lipstick.

Forty-five minutes later, Nae and Mimi emerged with attitudes. Every curve and every bump was hidden by those almost floor length moo-moos they wore. Only then could I see the family resemblance.

Shortly after they got home, Ms. Ruth left for work, not to return 'til morning.

Mimi and Nae were left alone to publicly demonstrate how that night's bible study lesson impacted them.

"Hey, Reggie. Hey, Shaun. Hey, Byron. Hey, Jon Jon. Where y'all goin'?"

"To the trails."

"Can we come?"

Chapter Eight

Nae knew Trickey liked her, which made it easy to get over on him. "Let's go to the store right quick," she suggested.

"But I don't have any money," I said.

"So?" Mimi said.

Nae slapped her arm. "I got you, Trek."

Once at the store, ol' boy greeted us.

"Well, looka here." He beamed so bright from the mouth I thought I'd go blind.

"Trickey! What's happenin', baby?"

So that's his name.

"It's all about you, boo. It's all about you."

Mimi and her friend, Niecy, disappeared down the candy aisle.

Nae reached across the counter to hug Trickey. As her petite arms stretched over to embrace his rolls, he grabbed her breasts.

"Aye, stop boy!" She popped the side of his balding head.

"You know you like when I do that. Come here, let me talk to you for a minute."

Nae propped herself up in a comfortable position allowing her breast to rest on the counter. Trickey also leaned forward whispering in her ear. At first I was curious about what he was saying to her. Then I noticed Trickey's hands inside Nae's tube top.

Mimi and Niecy walked out the store without a word to anyone.

Seconds later, "Trickey, baby, I gotta go."

"What? Come on, Nae. I...I ain't done yet." He looked like he might cry.

"Hey...hey," she said pulling back, "tell ya' what. How 'bout I stop by yo' place later on."

"Unh-huh, that's what you said last time."

"Baby, it wasn't my fault mama didn't go to work that night."

I could tell he still didn't believe her. "Yea...ah-ight."

Nae blew him a kiss and we left.

"Do you like him?" I asked trying to make sense of what had just happened.

"Girl, please. I'd blow his mind."

Trickey, what's in a name?

We turned the corner to find Mimi and Niecy emptying stuff from their shorts, tops, socks, everywhere. They amazed me with their creative solutions for storing loot. Regular criminal masterminds.

Mimi rationed the spoil. "Here's some for you, Niecy, for me, for you, Trek, and Nae, here's yours. Ya see what happens when e'erbody play they part?"

"What did I do?" I asked.

"You were the lookout, Trek, damn." They laughed at me.

I never went inside a store with them again. I decided it would be better for me to find a boyfriend.

Being down with the Village hoes wasn't all bad though. While not the smartest decision on my part, hanging with them had its advantages.

Suddenly, I had no fear. No more hiding out in my apartment. No more silent treatment from the kids in the square. Everywhere my foot stepped I heard, "Hey, Trekela!"

"What's up, Tre!"

"Woo hoo, Trekela, hey nah!"

And I always spoke back. "Hey nah!"

Nae and Mimi lifted me above mere child's play. The closer I got to them and my 11th birthday, the closer I got to womanhood.

Chapter Nine

Nae and Mimi had no boundaries.

Once Mimi and I passed the washateria and heard funny noises. Mimi stopped. "Shhh. You hear that?"

"Yeah. It sounds like a woman in pain."

My heart raced as I remembered Keisha.

"Mimi, let's peek in to see if she needs our help." Mimi nodded okay. She went in front of me, squatting down and waddling like a duck towards the washateria opening. I followed close on her heels. My stomach hurt so bad I was scared I'd dump on myself. The closer we got to the opening the louder the woman's groans became. Except now, we heard a man's voice, too.

"You like that baby?" he said.

"I can't get enough of you," said a deeper voice.

What the hell?

"Come on, man, it's my turn now. You had enuff already," said a third voice.

I attempted to come alongside Mimi who now had full view. She turned to face me, her eyes wide as her gap. If whatever she saw was a shock to her, the sight might kill me.

"Trek, I think you right. She need our help," Mimi said. She stood to straighten her clothes and give her hair a few strokes with the comb sticking out in the back of her head. She sashayed her narrow behind right in the middle of the washateria.

"Which one is mine?" she said using her finger to seductively circle her nipple.

I heard a few gasps, then, "Which one can you handle?"

"Whichever you wanna spare."

"I'ma tell mama."

There were giggles and then Mimi disappeared into the pleasure corner. I heard laughter and hands slapping.

It was either Mimi slapping the mystery woman's hand, or the three brothas celebrating the arrival of fresh meat.

The smacking and groaning recommenced. Struggling to decide if I should stay and watch or run, I continued to peek through the wood cracks.

Then, I heard Mimi speak out. "Wait. Our other friend is standing outside. Trek!"

My decision was made. I took off.

Oblivious to everything around me, I ran and didn't stop running until I reached #1258-D. Rushing in, I slammed and locked the door. Ned sat in the living room watching TV, eating a jelly sandwich. He looked up for a minute, then back down to the TV.

Good. He didn't notice anything suspicious. I sat down on the couch trying to get into his silly cartoon. But my head was spinning.

By process of elimination, I voted Nae the likely candidate for the mystery woman. I couldn't believe her and Mimi. Needing time alone to think, I retreated to my bedroom and remembered why I never spent time in it. Ned threw his junk all over. I hated sharing with his nasty behind. I took a seat on the bottom bunk. Were they still in there? I went to the window and peeked through the curtains. Just beyond where Van, Steph and Angie jumped rope, I saw a man come out of the washateria, tightening the drawstring on his pants. He stopped and pointed to his left towards my window.

Aye! I shut the curtain praying he didn't see me. Seconds later, I peeked out again to see Vanessa and Stephanie walk towards him.

I closed the curtain again. I didn't see nothing. I don't know nothing.

I went back to the living room and found a way to make those cartoons the funniest thing this side of Flip Wilson.

After that stunt, I wanted as little as possible to do with Nae and Mimi.

Whenever they knocked on our door and asked for me, Ned told them I was on punishment and couldn't leave my room. One time I overheard them say I must've really done it to be on punishment this long.

After a while, I lost count how long I'd been couped up. Ned refused to block for me, and I started slipping. I carelessly forgot my fugitive routine.

Right in the middle of the ABC Kid's After School Special about a girl who ran away from home and became a teenage prostitute, someone knocked at the door. I opened it without looking.

"Hey, Trek!"

Damn.

"Hey, Nae. Hey Mimi."

"You still on punishment?" Mimi asked.

"Unh-huh," I said rolling my eyes, trying to appear annoyed by it.

"What'd you do?" Nae asked with red lips sucking a blow-pop.

"You name it, I did it." I threw my hands up to enhance my act.

They nodded.

"Well, you gon' come outside wit' us or you want us to come inside wit' you?"

Nae ain't slick. She just wanted to come in my house.

"Didn't you jus' hear her say she on punishment?" Mimi said irritated with Nae.

"WELL, HER MAMA AIN'T HERE NOW!" Nae shot back. Mimi rolled her eyes and looked the other way. Smart girl.

"Trek, we'll be gon' by the time yo' mama git here."

Like Mimi, I knew my place, too. I let them in.

Mimi perked up some. We did have one of the nicest units in the complex, if I must say so myself. Everyone had at least a couch, dining table, bedroom mattresses and a TV.

But we had an oversized floral print, velour sofa with the matching lazy boy recliner purchased at Foley's. Mama decorated our walls with choice pieces of special ordered Home Interior. The prize piece of #1258-D though was no doubt the three-piece oak wall unit with a complete set of Encyclopedia Brittanica with the gold trim pages. Mama used the middle unit with glass doors to showcase wine stems and other decorative pieces, like the bouquet she caught at her niece Shanda's wedding.

Beyond the living room, the apartment lost some of its snazziness. Ned's and my bunkbed didn't match our dresser. While we had a toy bin, we rarely used it. We found it easier to let the toys decorate the outside of the bin. Our bathroom's only decoration was the wallpaper that came with the apartment. Orange, yellow and green was a good combination, I guess.

Mama's bedroom was a lot nicer. Her king size bed with the brass headboard would be the perfect place to entertain, as I would later find out.

"Damn, Trek, what y'all got to eat around here? I'm hungry as hell." Mimi rummaged through my refrigerator and cupboards like a stray cat that ain't ate in weeks.

"Bingo!" She helped herself to all the peanut butter one slice of bread could stand. Afterwards, she pulled the pitcher of red Kool-aid out the refrigerator and set it on the counter. I watched as she opened all the cabinet doors.

What is she looking for? I tried to play cool about it, but between Mimi in and out of our stuff and Nae lounging on our sofa with her shoes on, they were on my last nerve.

Mimi carried her search for the anonymous object into the living room. Stopping in front of the wall unit, she opened the glass doors, pulled out one of my mama's wine stems, took it in the kitchen, poured her Kool-aid and sipped from the wine glass like she was royalty.

After she got her meal together, she came and sat down on the recliner and propped her feet up.

"Did you tell Trek about the party?" Mimi said, her words muffled by the peanut butter sticking to the roof of her mouth.

"Oh yeah. Trek, we're having a slumber party. Since me, Mimi *and Mary* did good in school this year, mama said we can have a party."

"We were tryin' to have a party that boys could come to, but…"

"…mama's sanctified ass wasn't havin' it!" Nae finished Mimi's comment. They laughed it off.

I figured they'd be pissed for not being able to have boys there. Slumber parties seemed childish when compared to all the other ways they "entertain".

"You think yo' mama will lift the punishment for one night? You gon' be right here in the square with all girls. Just ask her."

'kay.

Chapter Ten

No one contained their "school is out for the summer" excitement. Everywhere you traveled throughout the Village, you found speakers in windows or positioned outside the door. Bobby Blue Bland, Sugarhill Gang, Millie Jackson, and Shalimar all blaring out together created serious audio pollution. But I overlooked it. School was out for three months! Summer break was like consuming unlimited portions of a three-layered birthday cake. The slumber party was the chocolate icing neatly slopped on top and in between the layers.

People from all over the village crowded the square. I recognized many of their faces from Aunt Sis' complex. Everyone with a bike, skates, or two functioning legs hung out. Nae and Mimi made their rounds, joined by Chanel. Ms. Pat sat upstairs with her 'companion' and her company laughing and having a good time. Dee Dee led 'the younger girls' in a few cheers. After the cheers got old, they stood in front of the speaker tuned to Love 94 and made up dances. The boys tossed a football back and forth to each other in the kickball circle. I enjoyed watching the men and boys play together, both clowning if someone missed a pass.

71

"Aw, man, you should've caught that pass. We need to be out here wit' you youngbloods mo' often," Vanessa and Stephanie's stepdad teased Ned. He grinned from ear to ear and threw the ball back. That was a pretty good pass. Way to go, Ned.

Then my mood got ugly quick.

"Shed?...*HEY!!*" Nae, Mimi and Chanel bumrushed that fool like he was a superstar.

I couldn't believe that beety-eyed fool had the nerve to show his face around the square.

"Hey, Shed, baby!" they each said as they gave him a hug. He wrapped his arms around their waist and palmed each of their butts. I couldn't stand the sight of him. Leave it to him to come around and spoil our impromptu block party. Well, actually I was the only one who seemed bothered. I hated Shed. And far be it from me to stay around people I hate. I went inside to pack for the slumber party.

For my eleventh birthday, mama bought me a cute bra and panty set that could pass for a bathing suit. I planned to put it on after my bath at the slumber party and make a grand entrance. I wondered whether Chanel had been invited to the party. Probably so. Other than the Curt situation a long time ago, she'd never really done anything to me. I guessed I could tolerate her for one night.

Clap...clap...clap-ca-clap-clap-clap
Clap...clap...clap-ca-clap-clap-clap, dink
We formed a Soul Train line while Rolls Royce serenaded us with "Car Wash".

"Go Chanel…go Chanel…go Mimi…go Mimi…go Nae Nae…go Nae Nae…" and on and on we chanted until we said everyone's name at least twice. We even included Mary in the roll call, although she didn't get up and dance with us.

Ms. Ruth had to go to work that night. So Mimi and Nae's drunk Aunt Kitten chaperoned us. I was glad my apartment was in plain view. If stuff got too crazy, I'd take my happy butt home.

Aunt Kitten had a great old school record collection. We partied half the night to the original hip-hop hits - "Rapper's Delight" and Sequence Girls' "Funk You Right On Up", "Do You Wanna Go Party". I danced my legs right out from under me. We were having the time of our lives. Aunt Kitten hung right with us. Although 22 years-old, she acted like she was one of us. Watching her prance around in them hoe-like shorts wearing high heel shoes in the house, I finally saw where Nae and Mimi got their fashion sense. We were dressed for bed. Aunt Kitten was dressed for streetwalking. Still, she was hilarious!

"Heeeeeeyyyyy nah!" Aunt Kitten thoroughly enjoyed her music and her "beverages", both of which left her intoxicated. She wobbled carelessly around the living room, incapable of keeping the beat or her balance. Then….BAM! She fell out.

Mary sprang to her feet.

"I knew it, I knew it, I knew it!" Mimi jumped around all over the living room.

"Come on help me get her in mama's bed," Nae said anxiously.

73

Please God, don't let her be dead.

Mimi wrapped Aunt Kitten's arms around Nae's neck, as Nae pulled her up and clumsily walked her to the back bedroom. We all followed close behind. Nae laid her across the bed, removing her shoes carefully.

"Mary, stay in the bedroom with Aunt Kitten. Make sure she don't throw up or nothing," Nae instructed, closing the door behind her as everyone but Mary left the room.

"Nae, maybe somebody should stay in there with Mary to help take care of Aunt Kitten. I don't mind. What if Aunt Kitten has to go the bathroom? She'd be too heavy for Mary to carry alone."

"That's not necessary, Trek. Come on back in the living room with the rest of us. Mary can handle it." She locked my arm in hers, pulling me where I didn't want to go.

"It's time for the real fun to begin now," Mimi said as Nae went to the closet. She came out with index cards.

"Okay. We wrote out some pranks," Nae said, holding up the cards. "EVERYBODY will have to do at least one of these. When it's yo' turn just pick one, read it out loud and do what it say."

Depending on what my card said, I thought I may or may not do it. If I didn't go through with it, I knew they'd talk about me. My stomach was once again in knots, a condition becoming more common the more time I spent with Nae and Mimi.

"Who wanna go first?" Nae asked. No one raised their hand. Good. They were just as scared as I was, but didn't want to say it.

"Okay, Mimi, you go first," Nae ordered.

Cool. She didn't mind. She was so excited she could hardly sit still. Mimi pulled the card.

" 'Take off your clothes and run through the apartment butt-naked. You must keep your clothes off all night.' Ah, this ain't a good one," Mimi said disappointed.

"Unh-unh, that's the card you picked," Nae said.

This may not be too bad. My stomach settled some.

And sure 'nough, we sat there cracking up while Mimi took off all her clothes and ran around the apartment naked. To make it more exciting, she'd run up to us and try to touch us. Anytime she came near we'd scream and run away from her. Who in the hell wanted to be rubbing up against some butt naked girl?

After Mimi got tired of chasing us, it was the next person's time to pull. Mimi's prank wasn't too bad. I could hang. In fact, I could probably stand for it to be a little rougher.

Chanel agreed to go next. She wormed her way up to the card stack and pulled one, smiling from ear to ear the whole time.

" 'Take the person who just went before you in the closet for five minutes.' "

Whoa. Now I get a chance to see what happens when you choose to not do what the card says.

"Come on, Mimi. Let's get this over with." Chanel extended her hand to Mimi's butt-naked behind. They went to the hallway closet and closed the door.

75

What the hell is this? Did they forget to pull out the cards they were going to use when this was suppose to be a boy/girl party? My stomach hurt again.

"Y'all, let's move close to the closet door to listen to them," Nae suggested.

"Listen to them do what?" someone asked.

A couple of minutes later, Nae whispered, "Can you hear anything?" Nobody said a word.

Suddenly, we heard them in the closet stirring around. One started making funny noises. Then the other joined in. Nae enjoyed their antics. Everyone else sat quiet.

Niecy broke the silence. "Are they really in there doing something with each other?"

It was the longest five minutes of my life. They finally brought their freaky behinds out, wiping their mouths and straightening their nightgowns. Well, Chanel straightened hers. Then they stopped to look at us, then at each other, then back at us.

"Psyche!" they yelled and fell to the floor laughing. "Y'all we were just playing in there."

Thank God.

We all laughed. A huge weight lifted from my shoulders. I didn't know what to think.

"Okay, who's next?" Nae asked.

I'm ready to get this mess over with. "I'll go," I said. "Ah-right, Trek!"

"Trek, Trek, Trek, Trek…" they chanted as I mustered the courage to pull the card and go through with whatever it instructed me to do.

" 'Go outside in your underwear and tongue-kiss the first boy you see.' "

Man, what? I glanced at the clock. 1 AM.

"Y'all, isn't that kinda dangerous? It's late. What if some rapist is the first boy I see?"

After all, what other kind of man was out this late?

"Trek, we'll be right at the door watching you the whole time. Girl, ain't nothin' gonna happen to you." Nae's words comforted me a little, very little.

A million "what if's" came to mind. What if I'm attacked? What if the boy is ugly? What if our neighbors see me? What if mama catches me? That was a biggie.

But my supreme fear was losing Mimi and Nae's respect. So, I decided to go for it, playing the whole thing up to the nine.

I read the card one more time to myself. I glanced up and looked each one of them in the face. All eyes followed my every move. I walked to the table, laid the card down, slowly turned to face the group again, then…the show began.

I slowly lifted my t-shirt to reveal my brand new "ling-er-ee" draws.

"Ooh wee!"

"Do it, baby!" they taunted, howling and laughing as I continued my best impression of the Happy Hooker. Once my shirt was completely off, I did a slow, 360 degree turn with the t-shirt draped across my extended arm, modeling my pride and joy. For dramatic effect, I let the t-shirt drop to the floor as I walked with my head facing front and held high, and my hips rhythmically swinging and swaying side to side. The whole slumber party screamed. They loved me! With all the noise they made, I feared waking Aunt Kitten. Actually, it would've been kind of a blessing if we did wake her. Or, maybe not. Knowing her, she probably would have found a way to make this prank more scandalous than it already was.

I opened the door and stepped out into the wide-open night with unlimited possibilities. Everything was pitch dark and dead still, a big difference from the earlier scene. Lights flickered through the windows of only a couple of the apartment units in the square, but the residents probably just slept with the TV on. After all, most people were only a couple of hours away from getting up and going to work. I had to make this happen quickly. Being held captive in that apartment for one shame or another had gotten old. If I refused to do the right thing, I had to at least get smarter while doing the wrong thing. Nae or somebody closed the door once I was completely outside. I settled down some once I heard them opening the windows and crowding around for a firsthand looksee. No turning back now. Once I finished my scan of the square, I walked downstairs. I could hear the girls snickering through the window.

"Shhh, y'all," Nae commanded. Everything fell silent.

I walked down the stairs, continuously surveying the area. I'd never noticed how bright the moon was before. It lit up the square. In my potentially raunchiest moment, the moon was like a spotlight on me. I had to get away from it. Where could I run? My eyes darted from one end of the square to the other. I located a spot in the shadow of the shrubbery by the parking lot.

I looked up at the apartment then back to the spot. Yea, they could still see me. Cool. I ran into the shadow and stood there. Before I could completely catch my breath, a car rolled by. It stopped.

Uh-oh.

I leaned back in the shadow a little more, hoping to not be seen. It didn't work. Suddenly the red lights turned white as the car crawled backwards to where I stood. The window rolled down.

"Hey, lil mama. What'chu doing out this late, huh?"

It was Trickey. Maybe he was concerned for my safety.

"You lookin' to get into somethin' tonight? Hop on in here and let me 'tend to ya," he said, making vulgar expressions with his tongue.

"Come on, nah. I ain't gon' hurt'chu," opening the car door and motioning me to get in. I froze. I couldn't feel my legs.

"Trek, why you scared?"

How does everybody know my name when I haven't told them?

"You don' seen me at my job and you kno' where I live." He opened the driver side door to get out. This game wasn't funny anymore. I don't care what Mimi and Nae think of me, I won't go anywhere with this man.

Before I had a chance to scream or run off, he jumped back in his car and drove off. That was it. I decided to take my butt back into the apartment as fast as my little legs could carry me. As I turned to head towards the staircase, I bumped into a figure.

Oh God, please don't let me die.

Too scared to run or scream, I stood paralyzed. To my surprise, he didn't move either, just stood there holding the handle on his boombox, looking me up and down. Wait a minute. I know him. I don't know his name, but he was one of the older boys who lived in Crestmont. I'd seen him play against our boys in kickball. Hearing faint giggles and squeals, my fears settle as my bad girl confidence surfaced.

Not wanting to miss the moment, I closed my eyes and lunged forward, planting my lips firmly on his. Confused, he pushed me back. Finally, I'd done it. I could go back into the apartment and let the next girl take her turn. But as I attempted to walk past him, he set his radio down and grabbed my arm. Confused, I looked back. Slowly he pulled me close, never allowing my eyes to leave his. He tilted his head, closed his eyes, opened his mouth and gave me my first piece of tongue action. I had no idea if I'd ever see this boy again. But it sure felt good being in his arms.

Just as I started to get use to his kissing style, he stopped. "Follow me."

He led me out of the shadow into the moonlight. No one had ever been so sweet to me. I'd follow this man any-where.

He led me to the "pleasure corner".

"Oooh, –" I heard in the background, then other muffled sounds.

Instead of him pressing his tall, masculine body against mine, he placed his back on the wall and allowed me to lean into him, a true gentleman. I was free to leave at will. But I didn't want to.

His hands rubbed gently on my behind as we continued to kiss. Wallowing in the security his arms brought me, I kept thinking *"will anyone ever make me feel this way again?"*

"Baby, you feel so good," he said in between kisses, while his hands explored the rest of my femininity. I loved the attention. I recorded every stroke his hand made, knowing it would soon be over, wanting my own hands to memorize that moment for future references. Over and over again he touched every private part of my body.

Then the bra and panties became a stumblingblock for what he really wanted. Gently, he began to unsnap my bra from the back. I allowed it. When he touched my breast, the sensation was too great to maintain my composure. I squealed so loud, he placed his hand over my mouth.

"You like that?" he whispered in my ear.

He could touch me there all night.

He seemed content to freely roam my body at first. But it didn't take long before he decided to go for the gusto. He reached his hand between my legs. It tickled a little. But I allowed it. I knew I flirted with danger, but I couldn't stop. We were in the hazardous zone. Red warning lights flashed in my head. As long as my feet continued to touch the bottom of the shallow waters, we could wade all night. That is, until…

"Umph…" I muttered.

We floated into waters too deep for my surface-level swim skills. The fingers that before were pleased to tease my body's exterior madly searched for an entrance to the interior.

"Unh-unh…stop," I mumbled as his tongue fought to cut off my speech.

I knew I was in over my head. But how do I get out of this? What will he think about me if I don't finish what *I* started? I'd been a willing participant up to that point. First my body whispered 'yes'. Now it screamed "HELL NO!".

Acting on impulse, I pulled away from him, and ran like the devil. I tried to get to the apartment before he had a chance to see which unit I went into. I wasn't sure if he saw or not.

Once I broke through the door, all the girls screamed.

If it was a mystery to him where I ran before, it's not one now.

Before I had a chance to catch my breath, they were all over me, tugging and hugging on me, slapping my hand giving me five. I couldn't make out all the comments. Everyone talked at the same time. The little I could make out led me to believe I was 'in' and there was no ever getting 'out'.

I'd seen the last of my self-inflicted house arrest days. That night, I proved I could hang with the big girls. I now had respect from those for whom it mattered. Even Chanel was all up under me. They begged for a play by play account of everything that went on outside, from Trickey to the mystery man.

"Why in the hell are y'all's lil' asses still up? Go to bed!" Aunt Kitten looked a mess, her face creased from the pillow and discolored since we failed to wash off the makeup. And her 'horse mane' pony tail was missing.

"Turn out all these lights, shut that front window and lay down somewhere. Nae, you know Ruthie will be home soon," she said cocking her head down as the two of them shared a "you know what that means" look.

"Ahh-ight, y'all, let's go to bed," she conceded reluctantly.

Everyone grabbed their pillow and blanket and searched out a spot on the floor.

"Chanel, come sleep by me," Mimi said.

" 'kay," Chanel replied.

She had the prettiest smile I'd ever seen.

Chapter Eleven

After the slumber party, Nae, Mimi, Chanel *and* me
were inseparable. My crew. The coolest girls in the Village.
When you saw one, you knew the others were near by. The
biggest change to me was getting to know Chanel.

I use to think she had the perfect life. Beautiful, sweet,
cute figure, cute clothes, great smile. She appeared to have the
best of everything. None of that mattered since when all was
said and done, we still shared life in the square.

"I need some wang bad," Chanel blurted out.

"Alright, Ms. Thang. Watch ya'self."

"What'sup wit' you and Black?" Mimi inquired.

"That mother-…don't make me get into that."

"Tell us. Don't hold out on your girls," Nae said.

"Well, Kilo called me last week. You know he been
tryin' to get with me, right? Anyway, Kilo told me that his
cousin Peaches told him she heard Black got caught at
Tammy's house."

"Tammy who?"

"You know who I'm talkin' about. 'Tammy Whammy'…she lives over in Esperanza," Chanel said drawing air circles with her hands like that would help joggle their memory. It didn't help.

"You'll know her when you see her. So, anyway, he told me he was going to his daddy's house in South Union on that day. Well, supposedly while he was at her house her mama came home early from work and caught them in her bed. He ran out the house and Tammy got beat down by her mama in front of everybody."

"You owe her a beat down, too, you know that right?" Nae said matter of fact.

"Oh, don't worry. We wit'chu. If one gotta fight, all four of us gotta fight," Mimi said.

All three of *them* had to fight.

"That ain't necessary. I had already added, subtracted, multiplied, divided and left his ass like a remainder any way. In the meantime, I'm taking applications."

"But how will you get, ah, 'serviced' until the opening is filled?"

"I'll pull in the next stray who strolls through the square. My mama's working at the club tonight. The house is mine 'til tomorrow morning."

"Let's go hang out at Trickey's, see what he got going on tonight," Mimi suggested.

"Is today the 15th? Oh, hell yeah. He's a generous nigga' on payday. Plus, he got friends that drop by. They generous, too," Nae said.

"Count me in. Like mama said 'Don't give it away'."

So much for having someone to hang with while Nae and Mimi ran passengers through "Train Depot" in the empty apartments out back.

Most of our days together were spent either hanging out on Nae and Mimi's porch or walking through the complex. Sometimes they'd come over my house and watch TV or listen to the radio. We made up this bad dance to "Ring My Bell" by Anita Ward. Every chance we got to show it off, we did. The Village was our audience. The music could come from any-where- a car radio in the parking lot, a loud speaker in a win-dow, a boom box strapped to Kilo or Ronnie's bike. Wherever we were when the song played, we stopped and assumed position. Chanel led. Mimi staggered to Chanel's right and me to Chanel's left. Nae pulled up the rear. The four of us moved in perfect diamond formation, shaking rhythmically fine the best parts of our glorious little anatomies. We knew what to do for attention. And we did it well. Hanging out, dancing and basically having fun never hurt anybody, right?

Ms. Pat and that faggot Darrel cornered me one time while coming back from the mailbox.

"Trekela, why you hanging out with those girls? They bad news."

"She ain't lyin, Trekela. They got the worst reputation around here," Darrel said smacking his lips and rolling his neck.

"And got the nerve to be in the church."

"Sometimes the biggest hoes around call theyselves Christians."

"We just tellin' you this for yo' own good. Yo' mama work hard to have that nice apartment for you and Ned."

"What she gon' do if you come up pregnant?"

"I'm not doing anything that could get me pregnant."

They looked at each other. "You sure?"

"You mean ta tell me that them older boys we see you wit' ain't tryin to get at yo' stuff?" It sounded strange to hear Ms. Pat talking to me about my 'stuff'. She's a grown lady.

I lazed around the house the next day watching "The White Shadow". Someone knocked on the door. Please don't let it be the crew. It's too hot outside. The smallest pair of shorts and slinkiest halter top can't make up for the hell-acious-like Texas heat. Before I opened the door, I glanced at the mirror. I wanted to make sure there wasn't any crust in the corner of my eyes, or dried-up crud around my mouth. I brushed my hair up on the sides with my hands and opened the door.

There stood a lady about Aunt Kitten's age. She was a little taller than me. She wore a white shirt with white denim shorts peeking out from underneath which meant either the shirt was too long, or her shorts were too short. The shirt read *"Do not be afraid of tomorrow. God is already there."* I liked that.

"Hi, Sweetie. My name is Denise. How are you this hot and sunny day?"

She definitely wasn't from around here. She sounded kinda like a white girl, but she was very pretty, sporting a casual ponytail with hair she took time to grow.

"Fine," I replied, still a little skeptical about this strange person I'd never seen anywhere around the Village, let alone the complex.

"I know you don't know me, but hopefully that'll change," she said leading up to whatever it was she wanted to sell me.

Her eyes were huge and her whole face lit up when she talked. I'd never seen anyone talk and smile at the same time. For the first time since opening my door I noticed the pile of papers in her hands with large print on it.

She peeled one off the top.

"I'm a member of South Park Bible Church and we're having Vacation Bible School here in your complex's club-house."

So, she was one of those Jesus people. She certainly didn't look like one. I mean, she was cute.

At first I wanted to say "no thanks" and close the door. But that would be rude. So I let her finish her little spiel.

"We'll play games, do arts and crafts, listen to music and learn about all the things God wants to do in our lives. Did you know He created you for a purpose?"

Really?

"Yes, Sweetie, He sure did," she said obviously reading my face or hearing my thoughts. Maybe God told her. She seemed to know Him like that.

"Why don't you take the flyer and plan to meet us at the clubhouse next Monday at 6:00 PM."

"Okay," I offered quietly, still unsure about if I'd go, but didn't want to let on. "How much does it cost?"

"By attending VBS, I promise you'll experience something money can't buy. That's why it's free!" she said as she playfully pinched my nose. I couldn't hold back my smile. I liked her. I liked her style.

"What's your name?"

"Trekela."

"Well, Miss Trekela, can I expect to see your beautiful face in the place?"

Wow, she thinks I'm beautiful.

"Unh-huh," I lied. At least, I thought I lied. Actually it would only be a lie if I didn't go.

"Okay, I'll be looking for you. Me and several people from my church will mill around the complex today passing out these fliers to other kids here. Tell your little friends about it, too. The more, the merrier," she said as she walked next door to Kayla and lil' Mike's apartment.

After closing the front door, a few seconds later I heard her knocking on their door. They're probably not home from daycare yet.

I placed the flyer on the coffee table. It might not be a bad thing to go at least once just to check it out.

Before I got good and comfortable, someone else knocked on the door. Just as I reached for the knob, my phone rang. All this activity at one time. I peeked out the curtains. Damn.

I opened the door.

"Hey, Trek-Trek." Nae politely passed by me, inviting herself into my house. As usual, Mimi and Chanel strolled in behind her.

Nae's lips were red, Chanel's purple and Mimi's were missing some color and slightly pouty from the ghetto sustenance of watermelon and grape blowpops and sour pickles.

"Hey, y'all. Come on in," I remarked sarcastically. My phone still rang.

I made a mad dash hoping the caller was still there. I picked up the receiver.

Out of breath, I answered. "Hello?"

"What'chu doing over there?" It was Aunt Sis. I could hear the concern in her voice.

"Hey, Auntie," I said, stretching the phone cord into the living room with my index finger over my mouth to signal the crew to shut up. I didn't want my auntie to hear voices in the background, then go tell mama I had company in the house while she wasn't there.

"I asked you what'chu was doing? Why you outta breath?"

"Oh, 'cause I was outside when I heard the phone ring and was trying to get to it before you hung up."

"Unh-huh…whatever. Look, what'chu doin' later on today?"

Now what did *she* want?

"Nothin' really. Just hanging out with my friends."

"Why don' you come over here and keep Piggy company for me?"

Man, I knew she wanted something. Piggy was her boyfriend's daughter. She was 11, too, but too quiet for me. I hated sitting around with her. She never talked.

91

As friendly as I was, I still couldn't get her to loosen up. But that didn't matter.

"Sure, Auntie. I'll be over there later on." I can't let down Aunt Sis. I love her.

"Ah-ight, boo. Where's Ned?"

"He's outside playing."

"Well, don't leave him there by hisself. Wait 'til ya mama get home befo' you come."

"Ahh, Auntie, he'll be alright. He's just outside playing right now anyway with all the other kids. So, he's not by himself."

"Hey…what did I say?"

I knew better than to continue the discussion. She'd won.

"Yes, ma'am," was all I could say before I heard her hang the phone up. She didn't even say 'bye'.

I went back to the living room to tend to my company, whose behinds could only be here for another 30 minutes. Mama would be home soon.

"Oooh, Trek, y'all got a nice house," Chanel said as her hands enjoyed the softness of our couch. It surprised me a little that Chanel was so impressed. I always figured her house would be nice, too, if not nicer than mine.

"Thanks." Turning to Nae I ask, "Look, what's up for the rest of the day?"

'Cause y'all got to get the hell outta here.

"I don' know. Let's walk through Orleans and scope out some action," Nae said, all wide-eyed at the thought of getting "some action".

"Cool. My auntie needs me to stop by her house."

"Let's walk the long way. I wanna stop by the sto' to get something to drink," Mimi said.

"Unh-unh, Mimi. We just left Sunny's five minutes ago. Trek, give Mimi some water." Nae turned to the mirror, brushed her hair up with her hands on the sides. "You have some gel I can use? I can't get my baby hair to lay straight." Nae apparently thought she'd settled Mimi's little problem.

"WHO IN THE HELL PUT YOU IN CHARGE?" Mimi jumped up.

Unsure of where this came from, we all stopped what we were doing to face Mimi.

"I don't need yo' pa-mission to go to the sto'!" I'd never seen Mimi, or anyone for that matter, challenge Nae.

"I didn't say you needed my pa-mission to do anything, HO!" By then, Nae was ready to squelsh both that petty argument *and* Mimi.

But not in my house.

Mimi didn't back down, and neither did Nae. At first, they remained in their same spots, yelling and cussing each other out. Chanel's and my eyes met. We looked around my house with all mama's glass stuff. Two of Foxwood's toughest girls in my house…mad at each other…about to fight?

Oh, hell no!

Right as Mimi was about to get in Nae's face, Chanel got between them. "Hey, hey. We can do both. Let's go the store across the ditch from Orleans."

Good plan, Chanel.

Mimi looked Nae up and down from head to toe, rolled her eyes and walked out the house. Chanel stayed behind with Nae, trying to reason with her.

"I ain't thinkin' 'bout her," Nae insisted.

"Come on, Nae. Y'all need to kiss and make up so we can enjoy our evening," Chanel said as she pulled Nae by the forearm. While Nae didn't put up too much resistance, I could tell she still didn't want to go.

"Trek, we'll be outside waiting for you," Chanel said as she led Nae to the porch.

I closed the door behind them and locked it.

I went to my bedroom and searched for something to put on that didn't need ironing. Through the window I could still hear Mimi and Nae out there acting crazy. They need to resolve that mess before we take off. Today is not a good day for drama. I won't have any part of it. I settled on a pair of white shorts with a navy blue tube top that gathered in the front to cup my breasts. I can wear my whiteboy tennis shoes with it. Despite the short notice, this will be a cute day for me. Once I had on my gear, I checked myself out in the bathroom mirror. I lotioned my arms, legs, back and chest with Johnson's Baby Oil. Two silver hoop earrings, a few dabs of gel to smooth the edges on the sides and back of my hair, and a touch of mama's colored lip-gloss finished off my look. I'm ready to go.

By the time I got outside, things had calmed down some. As we headed towards the trails, I passed Ned shooting marbles in front of Malcolm's apartment with some of the other little boys.

"Ned!" He looked up. "Tell mama I went over to Aunt Sis' house." He nodded and refocused on his game.

As we were leaving the square, I saw Denise standing outside Lynette's apartment, talking to her mama. Before I could look away, she spotted me. Embarrassed somewhat by her seeing me walking with these hoes, I smiled sheepishly. She did a double take when she saw me, shot the crew a quick glance, then smiled.

"I'll see you next Monday, Trekela!" she yelled and waved. Lynette's mama stood in the doorway shaking her head, looking at us with disgust and contempt.

Part of me wished she hadn't spoke to me in front of Nae and them. But I couldn't ignore her.

"Okay," I said quietly. I walked with my eyes looking to the ground until we were out of her view. No one said anything to me right off about it. But when we reached the trail, Nae turned to me.

"Wasn't that the lady from that church up the street?"

"Yea." I wasn't in the mood to have some deep religious talk with her right now.

"Hmph," she responded.

Chapter Twelve

We walked without talking for most of the trek. After we crossed the field next to the church, Nae broke the silence by coughing and clearing her throat.

"Damn I'm thirsty." Mimi, Chanel and I looked at each other, then fell to the ground laughing. Nae conceded.

Mimi's chip fell from her shoulder as she walked up to Nae from behind and grabbed her around the waist.

"I don't know what cha'll laughing at. Stop, Mimi", she said trying to hide her smile. The love returned.

It took forever, but we finally reached the store. As we headed in, two girls were coming out, one older and one about my age. Nae held the door open from behind it. Mimi, Chanel and me got behind Nae waiting on them to come out. We couldn't see if anyone else was following them. The door was decorated with oversized advertisement stickers for Kool cigarettes, burglar bars, as well as homemade signs advising *"No more than 3 students at time."* Since school was out, I guessed it was okay for the four of us to go in together.

When no one else came out, Nae stepped from behind the door and went into the store. Mimi and Chanel followed.

As I went in, I heard, "Trekela Baden!"

I turned around. "Robin Jones? Heeeeyyyyy!" I ran to her and we hugged and screamed like we hadn't seen each other in years. Robin was my best friend…at school. And I missed her terribly, even though school had only been out a few weeks.

"Trekela, girl, what is this you got on?" she asked as she frowned, grabbed my arm, held it up and 'ballerina turned' me 360 degrees.

I shifted the conversation from me back on to her.

"Look at me? Look at you and your little braids and beads and stuff. Your braids are so cute. Who did them? How long did it take?" I asked running my fingers through them, enjoying the clicking sounds as they knocked together.

"Shasta," she said, pointing three cars over to the left.

Shasta waved. "Hey Miss Trekela."

"Hey, Shasta," I waved back enthusiastically at Robin's big sister.

Robin and I sat on the curb and talked and laughed, then talked some more. Sitting there with her reminded me of how different my school and home life were. We reminisced about the school year that just passed and talked anxiously about going to the sixth grade. Our greatest fear was getting Mrs. Holster as our teacher. Periodically, I looked over at Shasta to make sure I wasn't holding them up.

Suddenly, she sat up. "Robin, it's time to go." Robin was in the middle of a sentence and didn't hear her.

Something was wrong. Shasta looked nervously behind Robin and me, then back at the ground real quick. I turned around. The crew was coming out the store, led by Nae. Just that fast, I'd forgotten who I was with. They appeared to be minding their own business. Nothing seemed out of order. Nae sipped her Cherry Icee through a super-long straw. Mimi and Chanel shared a Coke Icee.

My stomach knotted. I preferred to sit with Robin than roll with those trouble magnets.

"Trek, you ready?" Nae asked, lifting the lid from her Icee to drink it straight from the cup.

I cut my eyes back to Shasta who tried not to make eye contact with anyone. "Y'all go 'head. I'll catch up to you before you get to Orleans."

I tried to say it in a way where it seemed I was too into my conversation with Robin to leave at that time.

Nae looked at Robin with her lip turned up, then over to Shasta. "Hmph." With that, they walked off.

Once out of sight, Shasta bolted to the curb.

"Trekela, how well do you know LaNaesha?"

Who?

"Her real name is LaNaesha, but everybody calls her 'Nae'," she said, obviously reading my face.

"She lives in my complex, in my square."

Shasta scared me. She acted like Nae was an ax murderer. It turned out she knew Nae from school, where she was known for getting into fights and sexing boys in the boys restroom, which she also did at home. That was no secret.

99

But it was nice to know whether at school or home, she stayed the same.

I knew Nae was a ho'.

"Robin and Trekela, I want you to hear me on something."

I'd never seen Shasta look so serious.

"Watch who you become friends with. People make assumptions about you based on who you hang with. I know you are good girls. But none of that matters if you build relationships with raggedy people, you understand?"

She addressed her comments to both Robin and me. But I knew her advice was for me alone. Living in a three-bedroom home with their mama and daddy in a neighborhood on the outskirts of the Village, what opportunities did Robin have to run into people like Nae, Mimi and Chanel? Still, I appreciated Shasta's approach.

We talked until the sun went down. I wanted to distance myself from the crew. The longer I hung with Robin and Shasta, the better my chances of permanently losing the crew.

Shasta offered to drop me off at Auntie's.

"I get the front seat," Robin said running to the front side passenger's door, hanging onto the handle.

She'd get no argument from me. I was just glad to have a ride. I climbed into the back seat, stepping over their dad's work papers.

The trip would have been faster had I simply walked the steel pipe over the ditch. I knew crossing it was dangerous. Since it kept me from having to walk all the way around the median, I figured it was worth the risk. Still, I was glad to have a ride. In fact, I wished it were longer.

We pulled in front of the Orleans. Shasta stopped at the guard's shack and asked if she could drop me off. The guard waved her through.   She pulled up to the section closest to the front entrance, put the car in park, but left the car running.

That was my cue.

I turned to Robin. "Hey, girl. It was good seeing you." I paused to find the courage to continue. "Say, maybe I can come hang out at your house sometime this summer." They were taking too long to extend the invitation themselves.

"I'll ask mama and daddy," Robin said turning to Shasta for approval. Shasta nodded and smiled. Robin and me squealed as she reached over the front seat to give me a contorted hug.

When she let me go, I reached for Shasta and gave her an awkward hug from behind. I grabbed her neck so tight she gagged. "Thank you, Shasta! I love you."

Both Shasta and Robin sat quiet. I hoped they were still breathing. At that moment, I wished desperately to rewind and erase my last comment. Without looking at anyone or saying anything else, I exited the car as fast as I could, crumpling the papers I tried to protect before. I darted through the first breezeway and stood paralyzed with my back against the wall. My chest heaved in and out. I was out of breath. After waiting a couple of minutes, I peeked around the corner. I could see the red taillights of their car with the signal light flashing to the right. They turned out the driveway and were gone. I took a few more deep breaths. As I lifted myself from the wall, I noticed an old lady standing in her doorway.

She stood there with her brown, pin-curl crooked wig dressed in a floral housecoat. I'm not sure how long she'd been standing there. I tried to play it off by walking past her without looking at her.

"Bebe? Everything all right?"

"Yes, ma'am. I'm headed to my auntie's house."

"Well...is somebody botherin' you? You bein' followed by somebody, bebe?" She seemed concerned that someone was after me. The whole time she talked to me she kept looking behind me like she expected someone to jump out.

"No, ma'am. Nobody's following me. I'll...I'll be okay."

"Do you know how ta' get there?"

"Unh-huh. I mean, yes ma'am. She lives over by the pool."

"Which one?"

Oh yeah. I forgot where I was.

"The one by the basketball court." She thought for a minute, then shook her head.

"Oh okay." She watched me until I got out of the breezeway. Once I felt I was out of her sight, I decided to walk through the parking lot instead of the interior of the complex. After all, I was walking *alone* in Orleans.

I found my way to the parking lot and walked through the middle, not wanting to make eye contact with anyone. It's funny how the same groups of men could always be found working on the same raggedy cars. Why didn't they go buy new ones?

I passed by one where two men were looking under the hood giving instructions to one man lying underneath. All of them wore dingy blue jeans with the "Fruit of the Loom" underwear band showing, and sported either a wave or shower cap. One of the guys looking under the hood had a cigarette dangling from his lips. Watching him, I couldn't help thinking about how much trouble they'd be in if he accidentally dropped that cancer stick. He looked up and caught me staring. I turned my head quick.

"Damn, they didn't make 'em like that when I was young!"

"Say, can you be missin' for a couple of hours?" They all shared a good laugh at my expense.

Maybe I should walk on the interior.

As I got closer to Auntie's section, I saw a large crowd gathering. Wanting to postpone the dry visit with Piggy, I decided to follow the drama. The crowd pressed closely in until no one could move. I stood along the boundaries, just in case I needed to break fast. Most of the crowd couldn't see a thing, but we could hear clear as a bell. One of the voices sounded familiar. People anxious to see jumped up and down for a split second view. It wasn't necessary to see anything to know what happened. One girl messed with the other's man. Now the girl who's man cheated on her wants to fight the girl he cheated with. Pitiful scene. A cat fight over a dog. Where's the brotha'?

"I can't believe you had the nerve to prance yo' ass through here!"

"Fuck you, bitch! I walk wherever I want to. Now what?"

Uh-oh.

They stood there going back and forth talking trash to each other. Then I heard, "Somebody go get Fatso!"

"Nah…nah. Meet me in the hills tomorrow. That's right, bitch. I'm comin' by yo' square tomorrow. But 'til then, I just want to give you this." SMACK!

"Ooh!" the crowd roared. Before I knew what happened, suddenly the crowd bolted. Not asking questions, once again I joined the crowd. We all scattered, and I ran straight to Auntie's. I was ready for some down time.

I reached her staircase and jetted up the steps. I tried to beat the door down. It finally swung open. Auntie stood there, dressed to the nine, breasts half hanging out her wraparound dress, wearing way too much makeup.

"Trekela, what's wrong?" She stepped outside to better survey the area. Since she didn't see anything, she turned to face me, seeking an explanation. "Is somebody chasin' you?"

"Unh-unh."

"Why you breathin' so hard?"

"Huh? Oh, going up all these steps." She didn't say anything else, just smiled.

I walked in the house. "Hey, Travis." I went up to him and gave him a big hug. He wasn't that much taller than me, so his full beard always scratched the side of my face.

"Hey lil' bit. What's happening?" The kiss he planted on my cheek was brutal on my skin with that nappy mustache.

"Nothing. Hey Piggy!"

"Hey," she said, not looking up. Whatever.

"Uh, Trekela, you hungry? Come on in the kitchen," she said gesturing me to follow her. She never let me answer if I was hungry or not. This kitchen meeting ain't about me eating.

First thing I noticed was the phone off the hook. It also looked like they'd eaten already. Auntie stacked the dirty dishes, pots and pans in the sink. Smothered pork chops, her main dish, were still in the pan she cooked them in siting on the stove with a thin skin-like film covering the gravy.

"Trekela, I need you to do me a favor," she said holding my hand swinging it back and forth, not bothering to look me in the face. "Why don't you take Piggy out on the porch and play some games or somethin'?"

I sighed for dramatic effect. This was my favorite auntie. I'll do anything for her. "Okay. But where are your cards?"

"Um, look in the drawer by the dishwasher," she said as she walked out to the living room. I heard her in the living room trying to sell Piggy on how much fun she and I would have on the porch. I searched through her junk drawers. Bingo. To wet the dryness of being with Piggy, I pulled out the X-rated cards, the ones with butt-naked black Jacks, Queens and Kings. We were sure to have some fun now.

Piggy and I walked outside. We heard the deadbolt lock, as well as the security chain rattle. After taking a seat on the porch, I placed the cards in front of her. No reaction. Oh well.

We played a million games of Battle, Spades, even Go Fish. I could count the number of words she spoke. She kept looking back at my Auntie's door. I hope she didn't expect them to come out soon.

When playing cards got old, we sat on the steps people watching. Suddenly a crowd began running in the direction of the fight from earlier. Except this time, I heard faint sirens grow louder, accompanied by flashing red lights. The sirens stopped, but the lights continued to blink.

"What's goin' own ova' dar?" Well well well. Her country ass speaks. She stood to walk down the steps, but stopped. "You not comin'?"

"Unh-unh. I can see fine from right here."

People continued to rush toward the scene until a jam built up keeping anyone from getting closer. Whatever happened, the word traveled through the crowd and people reacted with anger, some even with tears. They cried out to God. But Piggy and I still didn't know what was wrong.

"Trekela...Piggy?" Auntie stood behind the door, allowing it to guard her nakedness. "What happened? What's all that noise?"

"I don't know. We didn't want to go down there and get into any of that mess."

"Good. In fact, come on in the house. Y'all can sit in the living room and watch TV."

Gladly!

It was good to be safe and secure on the inside of Auntie's house. Piggy could never understand how crazy stuff could get in a split second. Nothing good was on TV. I needed to call home. I went to the kitchen, placed the phone on the receiver for about a minute to restore the dial tone, then called out. The phone rang about seven times before Ned finally answered.

"Hello?"

"It's about time. What took you so long to pick up the phone? Where's mama?"

"Trek? You in trouble."

"Why? I'm over here with Auntie."

"Unh-unh. Mama's been calling Auntie."

"She had her phone off the hook. Didn't you tell mama where I was?"

"Nae's mama came over here looking for you. They not still with you?"

I was convinced I couldn't be in any trouble, until he mentioned Nae's name. For some reason, just hearing her name caused my stomach to tighten.

"Where is mama right now, Ned?" My patience wore thin with him.

"She's still outside talking to Ms. Ruth. You need to come home."

"YOU NEED TO MINE YOUR OWN DAMN BUSI-NESS!" I hung up the phone in his face.

Fifteen minutes later, Auntie and Travis came out the bedroom. Most of Auntie's makeup was gone. Plus, both of them smelled like they OD'd on Brute and Jean Nate. It would've been easier for them to just bathe. To clear their conscious, they decided to treat Piggy and me to McDonald's for ice cream. Auntie and Travis were more thrilled about the idea. Piggy and I just looked at each other. The phone rang.

"They'll call back," Auntie said. "Let's go."

Chapter Thirteen

We piled into Travis's candied-apple red El Dorado with the plush white leather seats, and headed down MLK Blvd...the other end...past the freeway...outside the Village. Auntie and Travis looked great together. They seemed to genuinely enjoy each other's company. I couldn't believe how happy they were. I loved the way they showed it, cracking on each other's mama and all. Piggy still seemed less amused.

We got to McDonald's, ate our ice cream and hung out like we had nowhere else to go. Then, Auntie announced it was time for me to go home.

Travis turned down Rosecroft into our complex. We passed the first section, the mailboxes, and the complex office. As we passed the tennis courts, my eyes shifted to the flashing red lights of the four police cars parked along the curb in front of my square. That's the spot Travis usually parked in for quick visits. This time, he parked in a space in front of the hills. My stomach knotted up.

"Trek, you in trouble!" Ned's words played over and over in my head. Auntie grabbed me and placed her arm around

my shoulder as we walked through the crowd of my neighbors, all of whom watched us pass by. None of this seemed real. Everything moved in slow motion as we waded through. I managed to catch a few glimpses. Dee Dee, her mom and granddad were the first people I saw. Her mom stood on the porch talking to their next door neighbor. Dee Dee's granddad looked me straight in the face and shook his head. Dee Dee wouldn't look at me at all. From a distance, I saw Ms. Ruth talking to the police. Mary sat on the top step with her head in her hands crying, and, knowing Mary, praying. Once we passed the washateria, we were in plain view to all in the square. Mama and Ms. Pat stood talking until Ms. Pat spotted me coming through the square with Auntie. She cut mama off mid-sentence and pointed towards me. Mama looked behind, saw me and ran towards us. The closer she got, I could see her eyes were red and her runny mascara left tracks of black down her face.

"Trekela!" She grabbed me and squeezed me so tight I couldn't breathe. Then she let go and stooped down, cupping my face with one hand. "Trekela, baby, have you seen Nae, Mimi and Chanel?"

I've never heard mama call me 'baby' before. "No, ma'am."

"Tre, don't lie to me. Pat, Ned and half the folks around here saw you leave with them earlier," mama said obviously high strung and extremely frustrated.

But I was telling the truth. I hadn't seen them since they left the store.

"Mama, I'm not lying. I mean, yea, I walked to the store with them earlier. But that's where we separated. They left me up there with Robin from school and her big sister Shasta. They were the ones that dropped me off at Auntie's. And that's where I've been ever since, with Auntie, Travis and Piggy." Thank God they were standing there to prove my story in front of all these nosy people. "What's going on?"

By now, Ms. Ruth came over to us. "Trekela, did they say where they were going?" Ms. Ruth's eyes were red and puffy, too.

"They were going to hang out in the Orleans…"

She cut me off. "Who were they going to see?"

"Nobody that I know of. They were just gonna hang. What's happening?"

"Tre," mama said as she pulled me off to the side, "apparently, Nae, Mimi and Chanel were in a fight and Nae stabbed a girl. That girl is in the hospital right now. If you know anything, now's the time to tell me."

Fuck you, bitch. I go anywhere I wanna…

"Mama, I don't know nothing."

With that, mama walked over to Ms. Ruth and told her she'd pray for the girls.

Me, Ned, Auntie, Travis and Piggy followed mama into the house. As we walked towards the door, I faintly heard part of Natalie Cole's song "Annie Mae".

No one knew about her past
Some people thought she wouldn't last
She was growin' up…much too fast

111

I looked around to see where the music came from. The darkness hid most of the people standing around. There was a guy standing off to the side by himself, obviously not a resident. I know him. I just can't place him right now. We disappeared into #1258-D.

Mama ordered us kids to the room so the grown folks could talk in private. I didn't know which scene to spy on first. Should I go to the door to see what mama was saying? Or should I go to the curtain to watch the square for more clues about what's going on? Before I had a chance to choose, Ned interrupted my confused thoughts.

"Ms. Pat told Ms. Ruth and mama about what y'all did at that sleepover...ho!"

In that split second, all the fear, anger and rage I'd been bottling was shaken and unleashed all over Ned. I leaped on him like a wild alley cat. His screams and tears didn't phase me at all. Like a leaf from a tree, I needed to be yanked off him. Upon hearing the scuffle, Auntie was the first in the room, commanding us to break it up. Travis came in after her and pulled me off Ned. Mama rushed to him, looking over his teary face, distorted by that hard cry he faked for sympathy. As I continued my struggle to break free from Travis's grip, mama left Ned to Auntie's brief care, then came towards me.

WHAP! Mama slapped me across the face.

"Ugh!"

Not wanting anyone to see me cry, I ran to the bathroom, slammed and locked the door.

"I HATE YOU! I HATE ALL OF YOU!"

I turned to look at my face in the mirror. I jumped. My appearance caught me off guard. Today started out as such a cute day for me. How in the hell did it come to this? From the bathroom, I overheard mama still going off. Auntie did what she could to calm her. I replayed the situation over again in my mind, trying to figure out when I became the villain to mama. She obviously had been holding some stuff in, too. From the bits and pieces of their conversation I caught, I was the source of her anger. Auntie kept saying "but she just a chile, Ann".

Once mama settled, Auntie tapped on the bathroom door.

"Tre? Can I come in? Please open the door, boo."

I could never resist her. As she requested, I unlocked the door. She came through slowly. "Lil' mama, are you okay?"

Without looking her way, I nodded. Before I had a chance to fully compose myself, Auntie pulled me into her bosom. Her gentleness melted my tough exterior. I wept bitterly in her arms.

"Tre, your mama didn't mean to hurt you. She just don't know what to do with you at times.

"I planned to spend some time with you before Travis and Piggy got to my house today." Holding my face in her hands, she asked, "What's this I hear about you screwing around with lil' boys over here? All the mothers here in the square told Ann about what goes on wit' chu while she at work. So don't bother lyin'."

"I don't mess around with anyone. All I do is hang out with my girls, that's all."

"Well, judging by the shit goin' on right now wit' *yo' girls*, I say it's time for a new crew."

"Mama hates me."

"Unh-unh, Tre. Don't say that. It's not true."

"I wish I knew where my daddy was so I could go live with him."

Suddenly Auntie posted me up against the wall and looked as if she wanted to kill me. Moments later, she let go and paced the bathroom floor, blowing into her fist before slamming it down on the counter.

"Tre, I know you not gon' sit here and tell me you'd rather live with the mothafucka' who beat yo' mama to pulp, tossed your lil' ass into the wall and had the audacity to request a paternity test when he decided he didn't want to pay child support? His sorry ass can't take care of his damn self. How's he going to tend to your needs? Watch what you ask for. Be grateful for what you got."

Reluctantly, she kissed my forehead and left for home with Travis and Piggy.

I stayed in the bathroom until all the lights went out in my house. Earlier I vowed to never leave it. But the thought of eating my food where people dumped turned my stomach.

I'm not sure how much time had passed. I figured mama and Ned were good and sleep by now. I went straight to the bedroom. Ned lay across the bottom bunk. In the dark, I couldn't tell if he was looking at me. Just in case he was, I rolled my eyes at him and walked to the window. I peeped through the left side of the curtains. This was so crazy. People were still out, although not as many. I wanted to yell, "Haven't you had enough entertainment for the night, you nosy mofos? Now, please take your asses in the house and go to bed!"

As I thought about how to do this in a way where no one would know who said it, and mama and Ned would stay sleep, Vanessa and Stephanie's stepdad caught my eye with his wailing arms. He stood on the sidewalk between his apartment door and the washateria, wearing his usual sleeveless muscle shirt and pants with the drawstring. While I couldn't hear a thing, I could tell by his body movements he was screaming at someone standing in the doorway of his apartment. He extended his arms full-length out to the side, then slapped his chest with the palms of his hands, then back out. Even from my apartment, I could see his muscles flex with each movement. He started to walk closer to the door. He stopped abruptly, this time holding his hands out in front of him. Then he ducked, covering his head as something flew over it. Another item came whirling out, then another and another. Finally the culprit stepped out the doorway and on to the porch. It was Vanessa and Stephanie's mother, dressed in denim gouchos pulled up over her fat stomach. Slightly on the stout side, she looked funny standing there, going off on him. She waved her finger at him and rolled her neck, which surprised me. She'd always been so quiet and reserve before, choosing not to mix with anyone in the square, just like mama. The stepdad picked something up from the ground and walked off. Vanessa and Steph's mama continued clowning him, even following him as he walked off. I made a mental note to get the scoop from Dee Dee on what went down.

I let go of the curtain, climbed in bed with my clothes on, and just before I drifted off to sleep thought, "what a night."

God, please protect the crew wherever they are.

Chapter Fourteen

I woke up the next morning to the smell of bacon and biscuits. I heard mama scrambling around in the kitchen. I could also hear Mighty Mouse cartoon on the TV. Good. Ned was in the living room. I had the whole bedroom to myself. I vowed to stay in bed all day. I didn't want to see their ugly faces ever again. I glanced at the clock. 11:45 AM. I continued to lie in bed until my head started hurting. Lying down too long usually does that to you. Plus, this junky room was on my last nerve.

And, Soul Train was about to come on.

I got out of bed and went to the restroom to brush my teeth and wipe my face. Afterwards, I walked in the living room without saying a word to anyone. As bold as I pleased, I went directly to the TV and flipped it to channel 39. I dared anybody to say anything. No one did. I plopped down on the sofa. Ned left the room without looking at me. A few minutes later, he walked outside with his football under arm. Mama retreated to her bedroom and closed the door. As I got up to walk to the kitchen for some bacon and biscuits, I looked down at the coffee table and noticed the Vacation Bible School flyer partially hanging off the table. I walked by, brushing it with my leg, knocking it off.

After eating breakfast and watching Soul Train, I fell asleep on the couch. I'm not sure how long I'd been sleeping when I woke up to Ned shaking me and calling my name.

"Trekela, some boys out there looking for you." I slowly came to consciousness.

"What?"

"Some boys out there told me to come tell you to come here for a minute." He went back outside.

Boys? Wanting to see me? Outside right now? I got up from the couch with a good, long stretch and yawn. I walked to the living room curtains to see if I knew them. I heard a radio blasting. But I could only see the back of their heads. One wore cornrows and had on a black tank top. The other one wore a popular black and gold Pirate's baseball cap with a mustard-colored tank top matching the gold in his cap. A third one sat a few steps up from them. I could only see his legs. They seemed real involved in their conversation. None of them looked around. So I never got to see so much as the side of their faces. I had no idea who they were. But if they knew me and knew where I lived, I must have met them somewhere.

I dug around my drawer and fished out a pair of cut-off blue jean shorts that fit real cute across my butt. They used to be a pair of jeans. But when they became 'high waters' on me and I didn't want to give them away, I made myself some shorts. I found a white tank top to put on with them. After washing my face with Phisoderm, I patted it dry, and used some of mama's skin moisturizer. It didn't make me look as greasy as some of the other lotions. I put just enough lipgloss on to give my lips a soft shine. My hair was a mess. I needed a perm bad. Until then, I wet the edges, dabbed on some gel and got Ned's stiff brush to brush my hair straight. Once it was as straight as it could get, I held my hair tight in a ponytail, causing my eyes to slant up like I was Chinese. I pulled out a dark blue ribbon and wound it tight around my hair, securing the ponytail in the same position my hands held it. I gave myself one last lookover before leaving the bathroom. Perfect.

Halfway to the staircase, I still didn't recognize any of them. I had no idea what to say once we were finally face to face. Hello? What's up? Hey now? Nah.

As I walked up, the one on the left saw me. He touched the other one, nodding his head to signal my presence. He looked up and smiled. I knew that smile.

"What's up, cuz?"

"*Milton*!" I couldn't believe it. I screamed and clapped my hands over my mouth. He stood to catch me as I jumped in his arms.

"Hey, Milton!"

Every fiber of my being ignited. God knows how I loved and missed this young man. The way he held me said he felt the same. And that felt great. Finally, someone's here that's in my corner. Milton and I bantered back and forth trying to catch up. The very sight of him brought back wonderful memories. So much had changed since I last saw him. I was a little girl then.

"Where you been hidin'?"

"Ah, I moved to the north side to live with moms for a minute. But she didn't know what to do wit' a nigga'. So she shipped my black ass back over here wit' daddy. It's cool though."

Snickering in the background forced my attention to the stairs.

"I'm sorry. Trekela, this here is one of my partners, T-Bone."

Oooh, he's a cutie. T-Bone shook my hand, trying to act civilized.

"The other oogly motherfucka' sittin' up there like he on the throne..."

"Aye, nigga, why you clownin J?" T-Bone asked laughing, covering his mouth with a fist.

"I'm trippin. Nah, but seriously though, that's my cousin Radio Joe." Milton said his name like he was announcing a performance by TSU's Ocean of Soul marching band. I reached my hand out. He looked down to lower his radio volume. As he looked up and we were about to greet, my heart stopped.

Jesus, it couldn't be.

"S'up, Trekela." He smiled a crooked "Joker from Batman" smile. He held my hand a second too long for us to disguise we'd met before. T-Bone and Milton looked at each other, but said nothing. I turned away.

I took a seat close to the bottom step next to Milton. I sat with my back against the stair rail in order to watch the guys and my front door. Talk about a crazy, mixed up bunch. Milton was still cool as a fan, respectful and attentive. He laughed like he loved life. I don' know what to say for T-Bone. That brotha used more four-letter words than regular words in a sentence. He was so loud, too. I'd never known a guy to talk as much as him. He was like a male Dee Dee. Ain't nobody experienced life enough to talk that much. I don't care how old he was. Radio Joe seemed pretty quiet. He never initiated any part of the conversation with his boys. He only responded to what they dished his way. I tried to not look in his direction. I couldn't be sure if I knew him. He played it cool like Milton, except I wished he didn't blast Blowfly's music in front of my house, nasty bastard.

While they talked and laughed amongst themselves, I thought about everything that went down yesterday evening. I couldn't believe how lucky I got. As I thought about it, I felt guilty, like I let my girls down. A small part of me wanted to go knock on Nae's door. The rest of me, however, felt free. Besides, if Nae, Mimi and Chanel were here right now, they'd take center stage, wearing coochie-cutters and halter tops, talking 'bout how they like their 'scow-scow-bam-bam'. That was their clever way of sneaking sex into the conversation. No. I held the spotlight now. Having the crew here would have cut into all the love T-Bone, Milton and Radio Joe showered on me. They would definitely bring a raunchy flavor to our otherwise cool set.

I could get use to this. I intend to.

While they clowned some more and we sat listening to music, my front door swung open.

"Trekela, come here." Mama and I hadn't said two words to each other in almost 24 hours.

I walked to the porch. What in the hell did she want? I didn't have shit to say to her.

"Who is that you out there with?"

"My friends from Crestmont." I said, crossing my arms and shifting my weight to the left leg.

"Well, tell your *friends from Crestmont* don't come around here with all that loud music."

I attempted to walk off, but mama snatched me back, pulling me by the shirt. She stared me down with bulging, bloodshot red eyes. Oh hell no. I ain't about to let her show out in front of my friends. Let her lift a finger to me like she did last night if she wants to.

My heart raced. My palms sweated. I had no idea what would happen in the next few moments. But I didn't care anymore. She hated me. I was prepared to see this thing all the way through.

We wouldn't have to go through none of this if she loved me like she loved Ned. Fuck it. I gave her a look like "what'chu gon' do?" She maintained her firm grip on my shirt.

"Little girl..." She hesitated, then, without warning, she let go and slammed the door.

That's what I thought!

With my chest out, I returned to my seat on the steps. I never did tell Radio Joe to turn his music down. I liked it at that level. It wasn't too loud. I could barely hear it sitting almost in front of it. How could she hear it from inside the apartment?

We continued to trip on each other. Milton cracked on Joe. Joe cracked on Milton's daddy. T-Bone and I sat on the sidelines laughing, especially me. I laughed so hard my side hurt and I had to pee. But I refused to go in the house. I'd rather hurt my bladder.

Eventually, mama came back out. Except this time she was dressed to go somewhere. She walked out carrying her purse, never acknowledging the presence of me or my friends. She scanned the square until she spotted Ned.

"Ned!" She met him in the middle. Her back was turned to me as she talked to him. I saw Ned shake his head and form his mouth to say "okay" before he kissed her and went back to his friends. She walked towards the parking lot.

Cool. Now I can go use the bathroom.

When I came back out, the fellas were about to leave. But I wasn't ready for them to go yet. "Where y'all goin'?"

"We gon' walk around. Probably go to the pool and chill out."

They not slick. They're going to scope some booty.

"If you put cha' bathin' suit on, you can hang wit' us," T-Bone offered. Milton and Radio slapped five. "Shit, think you can't?"

I felt uneasy about T-Bone's invitation. "Nah. I'm fine right here."

"Yes you are," they said in unison and fell out.

They pissed me off laughing at jokes made at my expense.

"Trekela, it was good seeing you, boo. I didn't know if you still lived over here or not. Now that I know, a nigga'll come through every now and then to check on you, ah-ight?"

"Promise?" I asked almost pleading.

"Scouts honor," he said, holding up three fingers the same way a small child would who wanted to tell you how old he or she was.

"Nigga, you ain't no scout," Radio said, shoving him in the back. They walked off horseplaying. Radio cranked his box up. Guess they needed more attention. Before disappearing around the corner, Radio glanced back at me and smiled.

I watched them walk away hoping to see them again soon. Except for our last few moments, I had a great time doing nothing more than sitting on the steps, listening to the radio with them.

Nothing was on TV. My girls were gone. With nothing better to do, I walked over to Dee Dee's steps. Yea, I'm desperate. It looked like some of the other little girls were hanging out with her, too. They didn't appear to be doing anything except talking and licking cool cups. I hope she had the scoop on Vanessa and Stephanie's people. Maybe she can fill me in on what all happened around here last night. Tara spotted me coming their way. She tried to look away real quick. She faced forward, but I saw her mouth moving. Without looking around, the others stopped talking, too. When I walked up, everyone sat quiet. See, that's why I stopped hanging with their childish asses. I ain't done nothin' to them.

"What's up, y'all?"

"Hey," they said together.

"Excuse me," I said cutting between the twins, Tara and Tasha, and stepping over Angela to sit next to Belinda, who sat two steps down from Dee Dee.

Yea, I was smellin' myself.

As long as they sat in silence, I'd do the same. It didn't feel right though. I remembered a time when I'd give anything to be down with them. It wasn't that long ago their silly asses treated me like an outsider for childish stuff. So much has changed since then. I felt lifetimes ahead of them. Dee Dee's steps were located directly in front of the washateria. A mother with two small kids waddled out carrying clothes across her shoulder in a pillowcase. I smelled meat cooking on a pit. Someone around the corner barbecued. A group of girls walked by heading to the back of the complex. They looked about Mimi and Chanel's age, wearing their bathing suit tops with shorts. I didn't recognize any of them. At least they dressed right for this heat. The puny trees planted by apartment management to beautify the area offered no protection.

I knew Dee Dee and them were jealous of me hanging out with older girls instead of them. Right now, all I wanted was for them to know I wasn't mad and to pump them for information.

The quiet act grew old. Being the mature one, I figured it was up to me to break through the ice wall that divided us.

"Where y'all get cool cups from?" Just as Belinda opened her mouth to answer, Dee Dee tapped her shoulder.

Belinda and I both looked back. Dee Dee put her head down.

"What?" I asked.

"Hmmm? Oh, nothing. 'cuse me, B."

Heifa know she lyin'.

Every attempt I made to strike up a conversation failed. No one had plans for the summer, or had been swimming, or was going to camp or their big mama's house.

Nothing.

My plan was to butter them up for information. But at this rate, I'd do better going to Nae's mama.

"Tar and Tay!"

The twins' mama headed our way. Every time I saw her, she had her hair in rollers. I wondered what her hair looked like without the rollers lining her head in seven uniform rows. Before she reached the stairs, they got up. She stopped in her tracks with her hands on her hips. They're in trouble now. I watched her fuss at both of them, then swat them on the butt. Both of them jolted forward from the lick. As she got louder and angrier with them, I thought I heard her say something about a fast ass girl.

I was the only one who snickered.

A few minutes later, Dee Dee's mama drove up. She got out the car carrying groceries. She ordered Dee Dee to come get the rest of them. As she reached the stairs, she started talking. I looked around to see to whom.

"I'm talkin' to you, Trekela! Don't be lookin' around. You know who I'm talkin' to," she said as she put her groceries down in front of Angela, standing there like she wanted a piece of me.

"You listen to me and you listen good. Damnit, keep yo' fast ass away from my child. I don't know what kinda shit you in, but don't bring it 'round my house. You understand?" she said with eyes squinted and lip pressed tightly together, as both of them pushed to join her nose in the middle.

If she knew how ugly her face looked right now, she'd choose a different expression. And if she understood just how close to jumpin' her I was, she'd get out my face.

But without a word, I got up from the stairs. She blocked the center on purpose. This drama was so unnecessary. I could tell she itched for a chance to justify tagging me. Make no mistake though. If provoked, I will clock somebody's mama. I narrowly squeezed by to her right. She didn't budge one inch. Angela got up from the step for me. I ain't gon' lie. I was embarrassed and almost in tears. But I refused to give her the satisfaction.

As I walked away, I overheard her telling Angela and Belinda she better not see them with me either, or she would tell their mamas.

Fine. To hell with all of them.

Chapter Fifteen

By the time mama came home, I'd been inside long enough to take my bath and settle in front of the TV. She came in with Ned. I looked straight ahead. He was excited about something.

"Tre, look at mama!"

Oh my God! She looked like a brand new person. I was still pissed at her for the earlier episode. The last thing I wanted to do was fix my mouth to say anything nice to her. But wow!

"You look cute, mama."

"Thanks." Expressionless and not phased by my attempt to act civil, she and her fancy new layered, stylish hair cut, retreated to her bedroom, Ned following.

Two can play this game.

The next day came and went with no frills. I stayed inside all day.

Monday morning, I heard mama leave the house to go catch the bus to work. I got up and walked to the kitchen to cook breakfast.

Hopefully, this would be a 'good scrambled egg day'. Sometimes when I cook them, they don't look or taste right. It depended on how much butter I put in the pan. I liked the taste better when I fried the bacon, then scrambled the eggs in the bacon grease. Ummm, so good!

Ned straggled into the living room, wiping his eyes and stretching. He walked over to the TV and turned it on. Oddly, he walked back to the edge of the invisible line dividing the living from the dining room and stood where I could see him from the kitchen. He ain't slick. He wanted some of my food. I'm sure he's waiting for me to offer him some.

Psyche!

I piled all the bacon and scrambled eggs on my plate, leaving him nothing to taste but the aroma. In his pitiful little way, he tucked his tail between his leg as he settled into the recliner.

With nothing better to do, I cleaned house. Top to bottom. I'm talking pulling crud from under the sofa, under beds, collecting loose change between the couch pillows, mopping the kitchen and bathroom floors. I even polished the wood coffee tables and the whole wall unit. Sprinkled Carpet Fresh throughout the apartment and vacuumed every room. I was possessed.

After I surveyed my hard work, I stood proud. The Carpet Fresh had helped a little to subdue the bacon and egg food odor. It was time to rest. I fell asleep on the sofa.

> *I am the baddest, the baddest to be,*
> *Mother fuck you and Muhammed Ali*

The stationery, vulgar sounds of Blowfly blasting outside my apartment could only mean one thing.

I ran to the bathroom to complete an abbreviated beauty regime. Brush teeth. Wipe face. Gel hair back in ponytail. Lipgloss. Shorts and tubetop. Baby oil on legs.

Out of the house in 4 minutes.

With keys in hand, I walked outside and locked the door behind. As I turned around, I faked surprise at the sight of RJ. He turned the radio down.

"Where you think you goin'?"

Quick, where am I going? Um, um – oh yea, keys in hand. I got it.

"I'm going to check the mail."

"Can I go?"

Gulp. "Unh-huh."

We walked through the complex, radio blasting for attention, and I couldn't have been prouder. My head up and my behind stuck out for dramatic effect in the shorts, I knew I couldn't be touched. For all the prancing I did, hardly anyone was outside to witness it. Texas heat cannot be matched.

After checking the mail, we went behind the office to the pool, where quite a few kids hung out. RJ and I stood behind the gate people-watching. Most of the older kids won't come outside until the sun goes down. They don't wanna get black, especially the girls. And they were the ones who brought the boys out. Right now, very little action was going on. But the few older girls that were out there, no doubt as baby-sitters for some of the little kids, competed fiercely for RJ's attention. As soon as they noticed him, all of sudden everything they said was spoken louder. I watched them find trivial reasons to come down to the end of the pool where we stood. As if that wasn't enough, they killed me bending over with their behinds facing us.

Oh it's time to go.

We walked back to my staircase. He's so quiet. I kept trying to steal looks at him. He caught me every time. The silence almost drove me crazy. We finally got back to the staircase. I wanted to invite him in. It was too hot to sit out-side. Ned's tattle-tale behind was probably somewhere close though. And he'd earned enough brownie points.

I really wanted to stay outside with him. But I didn't wanna sweat the sides of my hair. Gel can only straighten so much. Right when the dilemma got to be almost too much for me, RJ spoke.

"Why don' you hang outside wit' a brotha'."

'kay.

We sat on the steps. I'd endure the heat, but not the silence.

"What other tapes you got?" Blowfly had outworn his welcome.

"Nothin' on me. But for the future, what do you like?"

We have a future!

"I don't know," I said.

"Come on nah!"

"Don't you have some of the stuff they play on the radio? Like Shalimar?"

"Stay tuned." The total sum of his commitment.

I'll take that for now.

We sat on the stairs with brief moments of conversation, mostly asking 'why you so quiet?' 'I don' know. Why you so quiet?' 'I don' know'.

Unexpectedly, Milton popped in. Thank God. But RJ was a different person then. Suddenly, he was the life of the party. I had to admit Milton was always like a breath of fresh air. He brought life, laughter and joy with him. It was a privilege to be in his presence.

RJ and he cut up the way they usually did. Just between the boys. But I'd always get pulled into it. Without fail they'd insult each other by telling me embarrassing stuff about the other. I loved being down with them.

Rarely did I start a conversation. My role was similar to that of the studio audience. I laughed on cue, sometimes throwing my head back, other times bending over grabbing my stomach. I played the role. Because they were truly funny, it was easy.

Then suddenly their jokes weren't funny anymore.

"Man, she shouldn't've had her ass in there," Milton said doubled over with laughter in response to RJ's joke about some girl in their complex claiming to have been raped in the bike trails.

"Six-dicks Keisha all over again, man."

Keisha.

As we sat and talked, I noticed all the girls in the square gathering by Dee Dee' steps, all wearing dresses. Where were they going? I tried ignoring them. They walked toward us.

133

I pretended not to see them. As far as they could tell, Milton and RJ were the funniest guys to come through the square. Too bad they couldn't *hang* with me.

Our door swung open.

"Y'all hold up. Here I come. Let me get my belt," Ned announced to his entourage, dressed in his Sunday's finest.

I forgot. Today was the beginning of Denise's Vacation Bible School through her church. They stood idle on the sidewalk waiting on Ned, not wanting to look in my direction. Dee Dee played with Tara's beaded braids. Studying Dee Dee and them, I hadn't realized RJ tuned his radio to Love 94, that is until I saw Belinda move a little something.

"Girl, don't be dancin' when we about to go church," Dee Dee rebuked her.

"We ain't going to no church," Belinda defended.

"Well, God's gon' be wherever we going," Dee Dee shot back, rolling her head, popping her lips, loud talking Belinda. If Belinda wanted to one up Dee Dee, now was the time for her to take her stance to break out in a windmill. I know this display of exaggerated emotion was for our benefit. We were mildly amused.

"Okay, y'all, let's go." Ned came out picking his hair. It was strange watching Ned join up with a bunch of girls. I hoped some of the boys would attend VBS. Ned's sensitive enough already.

As he joined the girls on the sidewalk, they whispered something to him. He shook his head okay.

"Trekela, why you not coming to Vacation Bible School?"

The way he asked the question pissed me off. I know Dee Dee put him up to it. I refused to be embarrassed in front of my company. I wasn't having this.

Without a word, I rose from the steps and strolled in warrior fashion to the center of the sidewalk crew. I heard a few soft-spoken "uh-ohs" before everyone fell quiet. Milton and RJ, unlike with the other *little girls,* fixed their eyes on me.

"Hold up, man. Turn that down for a minute," Milton whispered in the background.

They expected a showdown. I couldn't disappoint them.

I cast my death stare on Ned. He looked like he suddenly remembered what I was capable of. He said nothing. Smart boy. I shifted my eyes to each girl on the sidewalk, standing there all cocky 'cause they going to be with *God.* I oughta punch every single one of them in the face. But they weren't my immediate problem.

Then I got to Dee Dee. Starting at her feet who I know stayed mad at her anytime she was in an upright position, I eyed her from bottom to top, then back to the bottom, and back up to her face where we stood eye to eye. I couldn't control what happened behind my back. I had no way of wielding my control over staircase gossip. But I'd be damn if she would blatantly front me out in front of Milton and RJ, and use my little brother on top of that. I mean, that's a double whammy. I can't let that go. The nervous tension in her eyes told me she really didn't want any trouble. Honestly, neither did I. Even though I'd never been able to trust her as far as I could throw her, deep down I knew she was a chicken at heart. Her eyes darted back and forth grabbing quick glimpses of her Garanimals crew who stood with crossed arms affirming they had nothing to do with her actions. She was scared and every-one knew it. Looking at her, I felt confident she'd never try me like that again.

Besides, she really was twice my size, and if I pushed too hard, she just *might* kick my ass. With one last look, I rolled my eyes and walked off. In a single file line and in the opposite direction, they did the same.

I returned to the steps and tried to figure out how to reintroduce Keisha to the conversation again. Dee Dee's simple behind wrecked our initial flow. Milton and RJ had moved on to another topic. But they knew something. I had to know the scoop, too. Maybe it wouldn't be too awkward since Milton knew Keisha and Erika were my girls. Forget the dumb stuff. I'm going for it.

Right in the middle of their bantering about something stupid, I interrupted.

"Milton…what happened to Keisha?"

Milton looked at me, then at RJ shaking his head. I sensed Milton would talk to me more freely if RJ weren't present. When I thought about it, before Milton came around, RJ was kinda cool, too.

But the two of them together? Forget about it.

Still, I knew deep down Milton was a great person. Shed was more of a buffoon than RJ, yet Milton knew how to rise above him. I'm sure he'd no doubt do the same despite RJ and all his jokes.

"Erika and Keisha are doing alright. They live with their grandma in Third Ward. They're cool." Milton looked away.

AND…

He reached his hand up gesturing to RJ, attempting to change the subject, when he caught a glimpse of my expression.

"That's great to know, but that's not what I asked."

He sighed real hard, looked up to the sky, then over to RJ.

"Man, don' look over here. She asked *you*."

RJ was on my nerves a little bit now. Milton looked back at me, then down at his feet.

"Well, I don' know what happened really. But they say she went to the trails, man, with six dudes, and…I don' kno' what happened after that. The dudes came out braggin' about it and shit. But Keisha claimed they raped her."

"That tramp didn't get raped!" RJ stood shouting. His tone got loud and his face frowned so deep, his two eyebrows became one. "First of all, she always waltzed her black ass through Crestmont wearing them tight ass shorts and halter tops even in the winter. Second, she knew everyone of them niggas. They see her everyday at school or around the Village. Third, Jamail said she let them run a train on her in them empty apartments out back by the trail to the Orleans," RJ said as he held his hand out and physically counted off each point with a finger.

"Ah-ight, man, shit. Calm down. You ain't gotta get all loud," Milton said trying to diffuse the situation.

137

"Naw, man. That ain't right though. T-Bone and the rest of them niggas almost got in trouble because of her lyin' ass."

Almost got in trouble?

I couldn't believe that nigga sat there defending those assholes. Hell, Keisha walked through this square bloodied, bent-over and broken with a ripped cunt and he thought *his boys* were the victims. I should've slapped his silly ass for making such a stupid comment. I wondered how *they* looked afterwards. Satisfied? Macho? Did their homies high-five 'em? Maybe they marked a notch on a tree in the trails close to where the act occurred.

Milton must have sensed my fuse was two-seconds from short-circuiting. While he didn't challenge RJ's story, he refused to roll with RJ's unintentional disrespect of me.

I debated to myself whether to walk off from both of them. If they justified doing that to Keisha, they could also justify it happening to me. I really wanted to say something. I couldn't bare the thought of not spending time with them. I mean, before this we were having a great time. The part of me with good sense pressured the rest of me to take small steps to simply walk away now that I at least knew what RJ was about.

Step one – stand up.
Step two – walk down the stairs.
Step three – walk in the house.
Step four – close and lock the door.

I wanted to stay, but I couldn't forget RJ's views. So, I stood up. Step one.

I stretched before proceeding to step two without a word. Right when I was about to implement step two, Milton stopped me.

"Trekela, I know Keisha was your girl and all that. But for real though…she was a ho'," he said with his arms extended out to the side, the ghetto nonverbal sign for 'that's all folks!' or 'there's nothing else to say about it'.

"Thank you! That's all I been tryin' to say!" RJ interjected with one last wild gesture with his free hand before he felt redeemed enough to sit back and gloat.

"That's why Shed quit her. He found out about all those other niggas she was screwin'."

Like Shed was one to talk.

"I know y'all hung pretty tight and all that. I figured you stopped messin' wit' her for the same reason 'cause I never saw y'all togetha' like I use to. Trust me, you did the right thing cuttin' her off. She was out there."

"Come on nah. Shed didn't want her tainted ass," Milton squawked like a lil' bitch.

I sat back down feeling pretty good about Milton obviously not wanting me to leave. I appreciated him for always being a class act. I rolled my eyes at RJ though. He chuckled to himself. Punk.

Now that the emotions weren't running quite so high, I chose to continue my probe for balanced information on what really went down.

"Okay – I hear whatcha sayin' and all. But you didn't see her come through here on that day, beat up and crying and stuff."

"Fake!" RJ yelled out, left hand simulating a cylinder cone used by cheerleaders when yelling to the crowd.

"You can't fake blood and bruises, RJ!"

Milton gave him a warning stare. RJ looked off.

I continued. "Just like you, I don't know what happened. I *do* know whatever happened, didn't happen because Keisha wanted it. And, yea, you're right – Keisha was out there. But that don't give no mofo the right to do to her what they did." I wanted to keep going with my defense, but my voice started to quiver and tears filled the corner of my eyes. I didn't want to cry in front of them.

"Hmph."

I swear if I hear one more sound from RJ...

"Are you sure it wasn't some girls that jumped her? I mean, Keisha was known for hookin' up wit' other girls' men."

I wished I could pull out Polaroid shots of Keisha on that day. I wanted them to see the hideous sight I witnessed. It still probably wouldn't have made a difference to them. They didn't want to believe the truth. Nothing I said or did would convince them otherwise. Disappointed, I allowed them to change the subject with no further argument from me. At least now I know what happened...or what didn't happen.

Chapter Sixteen

Everybody's mama one by one started to come through the square after just getting off work. I saw Tara and Taysha's mama walking up from the parking lot with Dee Dee's mama. They had stopped in front of the washateria to continue their conversation, when Dee Dee's mama spotted me on the steps sitting by myself with Milton and RJ. I saw her lips move, then the twins' mama turned around to see. They shared a comment, no doubt about me, then laughed. The twins' mama waved goodbye and walked towards her apartment. As she unlocked the door, she gave me one last look, shook her head, then disappeared inside her little sanctuary. I finally got to see her hair without the rollers. It was not a pretty sight.

Before too long my mama would be home, too. I knew I had to get rid of Milton and RJ. She'd trip if she saw me hanging out, the only girl with two boys. I searched for acceptable excuses to get rid of them without offending them and sending them away forever. I thought long and hard about how to approach them regarding taking their asses home so that I wouldn't get a beat down.

I decided to tell them I have to get inside and clean up before my mama got home. Just as I rose from the steps, I looked to my left.

Damn, too late.

Mama approached the apartment accompanied by some man who I'd seen around the Village. She looked at him as they walked, talked and laughed together. Maybe I had time to sneak in the house without her seeing me. I took two steps down and tripped, almost tumbling to my death. Milton caught me and helped me regain my balance. By then, mama rushed over to me.

"Uh-oh, baby, are you okay?"

Huh?

Mama turned me around and brushed off the little speckles of dust on my knees. "You gotta be more careful, okay boo?" I shook my head to play along with her little game. My face must have registered mass confusion because her man friend tried to mimic my facial expression as a joke.

Mama played his studio audience.

Once she composed herself, she introduced us.

"This is my oldest child, Trekela. Tre, mommie wants you to meet her friend, Chester," she said using her whole hand, palm up, instead of one finger, to point to him. He grabbed her hand and she lit up instantly. I didn't think she'd ever stop giggling.

"Hello, Tre..oh I mean, Trekela."

Very good, Mr. Man. You don't know me like that.

"What's up fellas?"

"What's up, Chester?" RJ and Milton repeated robotically and monotoned.

Once it was apparent to her that I would live after the tumble, she turned back to Chester. Now that she was occupied, I turned my attention back to my company, whom I caught trying to say something in private. Milton looked a little embarrassed. I didn't mind though. They were probably trying to keep me from getting in trouble. I think they knew I wasn't supposed to have company. So on the sly, they tried to collaborate on their stories. They were sweet like that, at least Milton was.

"Tre, it's time for your company to go home now. You know you're not suppose to have visitors when I'm not home." She still played that role.

"Yes, ma'am." So did I.

Turning to Milton and RJ, I shrugged my shoulders, said goodbye and walked in the house, with mama watching me walk in with Chester standing there in front of her still holding her hand. She watched me until I closed the door. I pressed my ear to the crack of the door, where I heard muffled conversation, then silence, then mama said goodbye. Anticipating her opening the door, I ran and jumped on the sofa real quick. But I forgot to turn the TV on. She walked in with smudged lipstick. Still floating on air as she proceeded to her bedroom, she asked where was Ned.

"I don't know. I think he's at the front office."

"What's he doing up there?" We continued the conversation, despite being on opposite ends of the apartment.

"He's up there with some of the other kids."

"He's up there doing what, Tre?" The irritation in her voice I'm accustomed to when she talks to me returned.

"I think he's attending Vacation Bible School being held by that church down the street."

Silence.

Mama returned to the living room wearing nothing but her panties and bra. "That's where you should have been instead of outside sitting there with them little boys. Don't let me come home again and see that. Now I didn't say anything while they were here 'cause I didn't want to make you shame in front of your little friends."

Yea, right. She knew good and well that wasn't her reason.

"You cannot have company of any kind when I'm not home. But you certainly better not have any little boys up in here."

She's ba-ack!

"How long is that church holding Vacation Bible School?"

"I think it's only one day," I lied.

Mama walked over to the dining room table. Good, this conversation is over, or so I thought.

"Tre – the next time you try to lie, be sure to hide the evidence, okay?" she said holding up the VBS flyer. "Be sure to take your ass up there tomorrow, you hear me?"

I shook my head yes.

Ned came through the door swinging and singing some song he learned that night. Apparently, he had a good time. He couldn't stop talking about Ms. Denise and how much fun she was. His clothes were ruffled and his hands were filthy. He talked about their dodgeball game and how he was the last one to get out. And he explained the reason his hands were dirty was because he'd completed the first part of an arts and craft project he'd bring home at the end of the week.

The next day, I stayed inside watching TV. No matter what mama said, I refused to go to VBS with the petty little girls in our square. Plus, I wondered if she'd feel the same if she knew what their mamas thought of me being around their daughters. I'm not going and that's it. I'll just have to take whatever punishment comes.

Since receiving a makeover, mama spent less time in her bedroom (alone, that is) and more time at happy hour after work. Cool with me. Chester had even grown on me. He slept over a few nights each week, which I didn't mind, except sometimes I heard them groaning and making the bed squeak. I especially hated to hear mama make all those noises.

RJ had become a more frequent visitor to my square. He still didn't talk much. Yet I knew he didn't hang around just because. One Friday night when mama went out to the club, there was a rare all-black entertainment awards special on TV. The forever beautiful Lola Falana MC'd the gala. I loved seeing all the famous black people in the audience or on stage singing *our* music and doing *our* dances. Make no mistake though. On that night, Michael Jackson was the main attraction.

Apartment 1258-D accommodated tons of Michael Jackson fans in Foxwood. People trudged in and out most of the evening, primarily Ned's friends. And there were others who I'd seen around the Village but didn't know their names that made themselves at home. RJ, Milton and loud ass T-Bone were in the house, too. I usually would have been nervous having so many people in there at one time. But there was something very special about that night. In a strange way, they felt like family.

"Uh-oh y'all. Here he comes!" someone yelled out right before Michael Jackson hit the stage. That was a type of rallying cry to all the stragglers hanging outside. All of a sudden, there was standing room only in our apartment.

"Hey, why don't y'all sit down in the front so we can see back here." They obliged.

"Woo! Check out his moves!"

"Man, forget Michael Jackson. Check *my* moves." T-Bone broke it down.

"Go, T-Bone…go T-Bone…go T-Bone!" the crowd chanted.

While all eyes shifted back and forth from the TV to T-Bone, RJ, who'd been real close to me all night, pulled me into my mama's bedroom and closed the door.

The lights were off. With the exception of the moonlight peaking through the curtains, it was pitch black. He pulled me close to him and held me. He stood about a head taller than me. From his stance, I sensed him looking down at me. This whole scene seemed strangely familiar. My body tingled from his touch. He cupped my face with both hands

146

and planted a kiss so tender I'd remember it forever.

"I wondered if I'd ever get a chance to hold you like this again," he whispered, followed by a kiss to my temple.

Me, too, mystery man.

My feelings and emotions were stronger than ever. Lots of funny stuff permeated my entire body. I didn't know what to do. I did know that I wanted to feel that feeling for the rest of my life. RJ seemed to feel the same way. The way he held me, the softness in his voice gave it away. He remained a perfect gentleman, planting gentle kisses on me while stroking my face and back. No roaming hands that time.

Then I panicked.

"RJ?"

"Yea, baby."

Baby!

"Have you said anything to Milton and T-Bone about…uh…you know…"

"Hey," he said lifting my head. My eyes finally adjusted to the dark and I could see him. "Whatever happens between us is OUR business."

Our business…

"I'm crazy about you, boo. I'd never put you out there like that."

As I melted in his secure embrace, I thought, "*Please let his hands travel to those familiar places just like the first time.*"

Chapter Seventeen

RJ came over everyday shortly after mama left for work. I threatened and bribed Ned to keep his mouth shut. As long as he got to eat whatever I cooked for RJ he was cool. The two of them would talk about guy stuff while I slaved in the kitchen. I loved the way RJ interacted with Ned. Ned was like a little brother to him. Anything RJ asked Ned to do, he more than eagerly obliged him. Without fail, everyday after I'd cooked and cleaned the kitchen, RJ would convince Ned to get lost for a few hours.

During this time, RJ and I played house. We'd go to mama's king size bed and mess around. We usually got naked under the covers. And, yea, I'd let him touch my thing with his thing. But he never put it in. The sensation we felt doing what we did was good enough. Nothing more was needed…for me anyway. Then we'd take a nap. I loved him so much I'd do anything with him…as long as it didn't hurt my body.

We didn't lie around in bed all day though. I'd fry him some bologna and melt the cheese on top for lunch. Most of the time, we'd lie on the couch holding each other watching TV. Occasionally, we'd walk to the store for soda water or candy, his treat.

Once while walking back from Sunny's, we passed a Foley's Department Store truck unloading mattresses and other furniture into Chester's apartment. Chester stood at the door directing them. I let go of RJ's hand real quick. I could tell that pissed him off a little. He'd get over it. Hopefully, Chester didn't see us. We watched him closely praying if he did see us, he wouldn't tell mama. Focusing so heavily on Chester we were caught off guard by someone calling my name from across the street. Chester looked over. I turned my head in the direction of where my name was being called.

"Trekela!"

She crossed the parking lot to meet us.

"Hi, Ms. Denise." I hoped she hadn't seen us holding hands either.

"Hi, Sweetie. Give love…give love," she sang as she grabbed me and gave a big bear-like hug.

"I missed you during Vacation Bible School."

Silent, I contemplated my shame, even though it wasn't entirely my fault. I couldn't get anyone to understand that though.

She continued. "I've been meeting with the apartment management about a weekly program. All the kids seemed to have had a really good time during VBS. If they give me the green light, I'll need your help. Are you available?"

"Yes ma'am."

"Great. As soon as I work out all the details, I'll plug you right in." Turning to RJ she asked, "and who is this very handsome young man?"

"Oh. This is my friend RJ." Trying to play down our relationship, I nonchalantly added, "he lives over in Crestmont," waving my hand in the general direction of his apartment complex.

"Well, my brotha, you're more than welcome to join us, too."

RJ chuckled. "Yea, ah-ight."

"Okay," Ms. Denise said facing me again. "Trekela, I'll come by your apartment when everything is finalized. God be with you," she said reaching for one last hug. I was less of a willing partner this time. But to avoid being rude, I hugged her back, not really attempting to match her enthusiasm, as if that were possible.

When Ms. Denise went about her business, RJ looked at me.

"So I'm just a 'friend' huh?" He walked off.

I got back to my apartment and heard the phone ringing. I ran to the kitchen in enough time to catch it.

"Hello?"

"Can I talk to Trekela?" the muffled voice said. Who is this playing on the phone?

"This her."

"Ho." Click.

I hung up the phone. Seconds later it rang again. I picked it up quicker this time.

"Hello?" Nothing.

"HELLO?" Still silent. Then, click.

The phone rang again. This time I just let it ring. I don't have time for nonsense.

For the rest of the afternoon, I watched TV and listened to the radio, dozing off whenever the phone wasn't ringing. Ned came in while I slept.

"Tre, don't you hear the phone?" Aggravated he goes to the kitchen to answer it.

"Hello?...Yea, she's here. Hold on a minute." Yelling from the kitchen, "Tre, telephone!" He slammed the receiver down.

"Who is it?" I whispered.

He picked the receiver up again. "Who's calling?" I hope the caller wasn't perceptive enough to catch the sarcasm in his voice. "...hold on again...TRE! IT'S ROBBBBIIIINNN!"

He didn't offer any kind of cover for me. Sissified fool.

I snatched the receiver from him. "Give me the phone. Hello? Robin?"

"Hey Trekela!"

"Hey...uh...What's happening?"

"What took you so long to answer the phone?"

"I was sleep."

"Oh."

I struggled with what to say to Robin. So much was going on.

"Why you so quiet?"

I stretched and yawned loudly into the receiver. "I'm still trying to wake up. Where's Shasta?"

"She's in there getting dressed to go to the pool with her friends. That's why I was calling you. Do you think your mama will let you come over and swim with me? We'll pick you up."

I perked up. "I don't know. Let me call her at work and I'll call you right back."

"Hurry up. Shasta'll be ready in just a minute."

"Okay stay by the phone."

My fingers couldn't dial mama's work number fast enough.

"Good afternoon. Shiner Oil Company. Charles Wright's office. Ms. Baden speaking." Waiting on her to complete her greeting robbed me of a full minute.

"Mama?"

She sighed. "What, Trekela?"

"Can I go over…"

"Nope."

"Robin and Shasta want me to go swimming with them. Please, mama?"

"I said no, Trekela."

"But why?" I asked dancing around the kitchen near tears. I needed to get away.

"'Cause I said so."

"Mama please. I never ask to go anywhere." Tears raced down my face.

"Tre, hold on a sec…,"

In the background, I heard a man's voice screaming at her about a report or something. Mama tried muffling the sounds to no avail.

"Yes, sir. Right away,…Tre, we'll talk about this when I get home. I have to go now."

I talked fast. "But it'll be too late then. They're getting dressed right now. Shasta is gonna swim with her friends and they invited me to hang out with Robin. Shasta will come pick me up. I just got off the phone with them and immediately hung up to call and ask your permission. Mama, please let me go…hello? HELLO?"

"If you'd like to make a call, please hang up and try your call again…If you'd like to make a call, please hang up…" I slammed the phone down. Suddenly it rang again. Hoping mama changed her mind I picked it up on the first ring.

"Hello?"

"You ho'." Click.

I can't take this anymore!

Before I was able to call Robin back, someone knocked on the door. I went to the window and looked out. Ughhh! What does he want?

"Tre-ci! What's goin' on lil' mama?"

"Hey, T-Bone." I squinted to disguise my teary eyes.

"You sleep?"

"Yea."

"Oh. Look," he said coming closer to the door like he was on a secret mission. "Have you seen RJ today?"

"Yea…earlier."

He rubbed his chin. "Damn. I've been tryin' to catch up to that nigga all day." Looking confused or concerned (I couldn't tell which), he continued. "Man, I really need to find him as soon as possible. It's not really a matta' of life or death or nothin' like that. It's just…damn."

He lifted his head and snapped his fingers to signal mental bells going off.

"I'll bet that nigga's back at Crestmont."

Well, walk your yellow ass back home then.

He continued. "His sister needed a babysitter so she could go to work. Damn."

As I watched him reason with himself, I thought, *"what in the hell does that have to do with me?"*

"Say, you think I could come in and use yo' fone?"

I didn't much care for T-Bone. The last thing I needed was for one of those nosy ass people in this square to see T-Bone going into my house. Never mind he'd only be using the phone. The truth can easily be lost on the finer points. I can hear 'em now.

"Girl, you'll never guess who I saw leaving her house today?"

"Who?"

"T-Bone, honey!"

"T-Bone who?"

"You know him. He the one that hang with her regular lil' boyfriend."

"What? Chile, she keep that up, she gon' fool around and come up pregnant. I don' know what her mama gon' do wit her."

"I know, honey. She's a handful."

"So…you gon' let me come in or what?"

I wished I'd caught the rest of T-Bone's argument on why I should let him in my house. The little information I had was too sketchy for me to go with it. I needed to get out of this situation as smoothly as possible.

"I can't let you use the phone. Our phone don't work."

Ring...ring...ring...

I closed the door a little hoping it would muffle the sound some.

T-Bone smirked. "Uh,...I thought yo' fone was out?"

I'm stuck. I opened the door and moved back, allowing enough room for him to come in. Before closing the door, I looked around to see if anyone was outside. The coast was clear. I shut the door. My phone still rang. I rushed to it. The faster I'd get the caller off the line, the faster T-Bone could use the phone and get out my house.

"Hello?"

Click.

"I'm sorry, she's not home right now...unh-huh...she should be on her way because when I talked to her a few minutes ago, she said she planned to leave work early...okay, I'll leave a message that you called."

"If you'd like to make a call, please hang up..." I hung up.

"What time yo' mama comin' home?"

"She should be here in about 15 to 20 minutes. Why?"

"Well, I wanted to be sure to be gon' by then. I don' wanna get you in trouble or nothin'."

Oh, my brotha', don't worry. It takes less than a minute to make a phone call. You'll be good and gone by the time my mama arrives.

He made his first phone call, but didn't talk. Maybe they're not home. He pushed down the button to clear the line for a second phone call, then a third. Instead of watching him dial numbers, I walked back to mama's room. I needed to straighten her bed from earlier.

Making it up all the way wasn't my intention. I mean, she didn't make it up when she left. Only one side was messed up before. Now both sides were out of order. She normally slept on the right side of the bed closest to her nightstand. I pulled the covers up a little on the right and completely straightened the left side. Puzzled, I studied the formation of the ruffles on the right. They didn't look natural enough. I decided to make up the bed all the way, get in it like I'm going to sleep, then get back up. Just as I was getting under the sheets, the bedroom door closed.

"Can I join you?" T-Bone stood with his hands behind his back, trying to lock the door on the sly. With a sinister grin, he approached me slowly. As long as I remained still he crept slowly towards me. But at the point he reached two feet from me, I jumped from under the sheets, ran across the top of the bedspread and leaped off the bed, trying to land as close to the door as possible. I struggled with unlocking and opening the door because my hands shook too badly. My heart pounded through my chest as I considered my fate. T-Bone raced behind me and yanked my hands from the doorknob. With the strength and stubbornness of two bulls, he whisked me around and forcefully rubbed his body against mine, pinning my hands behind my back.

"Stop, T-Bone! Stop!" I refused his kisses by violently turning my head side to side and pressing my lips tightly together as he attempted in vain to kiss them.

"Come on, baby. You know you want this. You know you need this."

"T-Bone, I'ma tell my mama. Now stop!"

"No you ain't," he said confidently, his body still glued to mine. "Besides, Chester got yo' mama and half the women over here noses wide open. She don't give a shit about you." The harder I tried to fight back, the harder he grinded on me.

"Please, T-Bone. Don't do this!" I begged. I wished I had a knife right then. Fuck that pleading stuff. I'd slice his nuts to make sure he never did this shit again. During this whole ordeal, I kept thinking about Nae. I'd love to have her *"I don't give a fuck"* courage right now, because my own failed me.

"Yea, Tre…or Trek…or whateva' name you want me to call you as we do what we gon' do…"

"I'm not doing SHIT WITH YOU MOTHAFUCKA!"

Struggling to breathe, talk and violate me at the same time, T-Bone took long pauses between each statement. "Oh, you don' think so, huh?…Keisha thought that, too…Tre, let me ask you something,…How many dicks you think, uh,…you can take at one time, huh?…Can you top Keisha's record, huh?…No,… I'll bet you wanna start off slow…How…how 'bout two, huh?…You want…unh…two dicks, Tre? Me and RJ's?"

My tears didn't phase him one bit. Breathing hard and heavy, while every now and then planting a kiss somewhere on my face, he said, "You gon' git it now. This what you been wantin' ain't it, baby?"

He succeeded in keeping my hands restrained with one hand while using his free hand to liberate his wang. He lightened his grip some to pull his stuff out. I saw this as my opportunity. When he lifted himself off me to pull it out, I kneed him between the legs.

"UGHH! You bitch!" The knee punch was so hard his thang got caught in the bottom of his zipper. He screamed out and fell to the ground.

Frantic, I unlocked the door. As I opened it to run out, to my surprise Ned was standing right outside. He looked surprised, too. Grabbing his hand, I ran to the kitchen and pulled out the butcher knife. Huffing and puffing, I stood in the kitchen holding the knife by my side ready to stab his ass. Ned stood trembling behind me.

"Tre, what you about to do?"

A few seconds later, T-Bone came out the bedroom, his shirt tucked too far down his pants, face wet from the pouring sweat. He looked over at me, then down at my hand. I tightened my grip on the knife. Shaking his head, he walked out the apartment without a word. We waited for about a minute to make sure he left for real. After that I ran to the door and locked it.

I walked back in the kitchen and threatened Ned.

"So help me if you tell anybody about this, I'll…" rather than finish my statement, I held the knife up. He got the point. Nodding his head yes, he pointed to my leg.

"Tre, you're bleeding."

I looked down trying to figure out where the blood came from. T-Bone never penetrated me. I bent my head down to see if I accidentally cut myself with the knife. There weren't any cuts or bruises. And I didn't feel any pain. I went to the bathroom to take off all my clothes. When I removed my panties, the blood seemed heaviest in the crotch area.

Oh God. I got my period!

Chapter Eighteen

I removed my washcloth from the towel rack, turned on the hot water from the sink and cleaned myself up. Opening the bathroom cabinet under the sink, I searched frantically for some Kotex pads. I learned all about menstruation at my school's "Girl Talk" session. We each got copies of Judy Blume's "Are You There, God? It's Me, Margaret" book that talked all about periods. My heart still pounded from T-Bone's attack. I hated him for robbing me of the joy I'm supposed to feel behind getting my first period. The shorts I had on were all bloody. I yelled out for Ned, just to see if he was still in the house. No answer. The phone rang. I ignored it. After wrapping myself in a dry-off towel, I went to the bedroom for some clean shorts and panties. I heard mama come in through the front door.

"Tre? Where are you?"

"I'm in the bedroom," I shouted back. I heard her pass by my room going into hers.

A few seconds later, she busted in on me. "Who in the hell been in my bed?"

Damn! I forgot about the bed. My head was too full of all the other shit that happened I completely overlooked the need to straighten mama's bed. The lies that usually flow so easily were missing in action big time right now. What could I tell her?

"It looks like somebody's been jumping up and down in it."

'kay.

I'll take the "jumping up and down in the bed" beating any day over the "I was getting some scow-scow-bam-bam" massacre.

She finally noticed I didn't have any clothes on. "Why are you naked?" She looked around the room, probably trying to see if anyone else was in there naked with me.

"Mama...I got my period. My shorts and underwear got messed up. They're laying on the floor in the bathroom." Before I could tell her I was looking for something clean to put on, she went to the bathroom to check for herself. I guess my word wasn't good enough.

"I couldn't find any Kotex to put on. I didn't know where you kept them?" I yelled from the room.

"Who been talking to you about Kotex?!" she screamed as she busted back in the room.

"I learned about it at school."

She looked at me suspiciously. "Hmph."

Okay, while she's giving me the third degree, I'm still standing here bleeding.

"Mama, I need some Kotex."

"I don't use Kotex. I use tampons," she snapped.

"Well, I need a tampon then."

"Oh, hell no," she said looking at me like I was crazy. "Wrap some toilet tissue in a wad and put that between your legs. Let's go to the store to get you some products." Still frowning, she left the room to put her shoes back on and get her purse.

"Hurry up and put some clothes on. I'm tired. I had a hard day at work and I want to get back and rest," she barked. "I know I told you that you can't have company before. But you better not have any lil' boys around here now playing in your poo-poo. I don't care if they are just 'your friends'. Do I make myself clear?"

So much for the mother/daughter Hallmark moment.

As we drove through the parking lot, we spotted Ned hanging out with a bunch of other kids playing some kind of game with Ms. Denise. When we finally got his attention, he ran over to us.

"Ned, mama and Tre'll be right back. We gotta go to the store. You want something?"

"Yea. Can I get some Pop Rocks?" His eyes lit up at the thought of being brought a treat.

Mama smiled with a fake frown. "I don't know what you see in those thangs. But, all right then. Stay around the house, okay?"

"'kay. Love you!"

"Love you, too!" She rolled the window up and continued through the parking lot. I wished we didn't have all these speed bumps. Maybe she could drive faster.

"Mama, why you buying Ned something? You didn't offer to buy me something."

"Are you serious?" she asked looking at me like I was from another planet. "Girl, I'm about to spend big dollars buying you feminine products, and on a monthly basis at that. And you got the nerve to be pissed off about $0.50 candy for Ned. Tre, honey, you betta get a clue...and quick."

Without warning, I broke down. I wailed uncontrollably for all the events of the day.

"Tre, grow up! That's nothing to cry about. Damn."

"I...ain't...cry...ing...about...that," I managed to say in between hiccups.

"Then what the hell is the matter?"

I knew if I told her the truth, things would only get worse for me.

"Nothing."

The hiccups continued, but the tears finally dried. At the store, I let her pick out what I needed, since she knew my coochie better than me.

On the way home, we stopped at the mailbox. Mama got out the car to check the mail. I felt my stomach hurting a little bit. The pain was like a warm, throbbing sensation I'd never experienced before. While rubbing it to ease the pain, I looked over to my right. I'll be damn. I scooched down in my seat so not to be spotted.

Mama got back in the car. "Let's go see Chester real quick while we're out." Her disposition lightened tremendously. The wicked lady disappeared for the time being.

Before I had a chance to object she sharply turned to the right, pulling her car over into the parking lot in front of his building. Before exiting the car, she checked herself in the rearview mirror on the windshield, then once again in the right side rearview mirror. She applied a fresh layer of lipgloss and rolled her lips together in that slippery mess. She stepped out the car, but not before giving herself one last looksee in the car window. Reluctantly, I followed.

Once we got out the car, I looked back over my shoulder. As close as I stood to him, he still didn't see me, too busy focusing on those three big-titty heifas surrounding him.

"Ooh, he's so nasty. Why don' you ever play nothing else?" the light-skinned one closest to him said, tossing her hair back, looking like Pocahontas.

"What I need to play anything else for? Girl, you know my man here speaks the truth. Come on nah!"

One of the girls caught me staring. The others turned around to see what she was looking at. I turned back around quickly, hoping he didn't see me. Before we arrived at Chester's door, the wind carried parts of their conversation.

"You know her, Joe?"

"Yea, somethin' like that…"

We knocked on the door. No answer. We knocked again. Still no answer. Mama jiggled the knob. The door opened. We looked at each other and walked in.

"Chester?…are you here?…" No response. I closed the door.

Plastic wrapping covered the shag carpet. His sofa lined the wall facing the TV set on the floor. Next to it were three boxes marked "entertainment unit". Mama walked through surveying everything proudly. I took a seat waiting on her to get through. What will she do if he comes in here and catches us? She milled around a bit longer then stopped moving suddenly. Placing a finger over her mouth signaling me to be quiet, she walked to the back bedroom. I don't know why she's telling me to be quiet. I hadn't spoke two words since we left the store. The pain in my stomach grew worse, and all I wanted to do was lie down. In fact, I thought I may as well lay here until its time to go. Shoot, Chester lay around our house.

As I got up to move to the other end of the sofa so that my head wouldn't face the window, I looked down and saw blood on the couch. I looked between my legs and blood soaked through my shorts again. Damn. I can't keep messing up my clothes like this. To hide the bloodstain on the couch, I was in the process of flipping the pillow to the opposite side, when mama walked in. Totally ignoring me, she flung the door open so hard the knob punched a hole in the wall. Unsure of what happened, I ran out after her. We got in the car without a word. Once we reached our apartment, she walked straight to her room where she remained for the rest of the night. I went to the bathroom to put on fresh underwear and a maxi pad. I refused to bloody anymore clothes.

I settled in front of the TV, placing a bath towel under me to catch any overflow.

Ring…ring…ring…
Mama'll get it.

Ring...ring...ring...

Ring...ring...ring...

Tsk. Waddling to the phone, I thought "*this better not be another prank caller.*"

"Hello?"

"Yea, Tre, put ya mama on the phone." Chester sounded upset. It's not like him to call here ordering me around. He'd better be glad I'm not feeling good. Otherwise I'd have to tell him about himself.

"MAMA...TELEPHONE..." I yelled.

I put the receiver on the counter before running to cut the TV down. I then ran back to the phone and quietly picked it back up.

"...and what the hell you doin' snoopin' around my apartment. How the hell did you get in?"

"How could you, Chester? Haven't I been good to you?" mama said, her voice cracking then going silent. She sniffled and blew her nose.

"Don' give me that soap opera shit, Ann. I'm not feelin' that drama today, ah-ight?"

"Why, Chester? *Why?*"

"*Why?* Oh, you askin' me *why* huh? Well let me ask you a '*why*' question, Ann?" he said, each time he spoke the word 'why' he mimicked her. "*Why* in the fuck did you come over here and leave a big ass bloodstain on my new sofa, huh? Answer that '*why*' question, bitch."

"*MOTHERFUCKER, HOW DARE YOU TURN THIS SHIT AROUND ON ME!*"

By now, mama no longer sounded like a bruised little lamb. She sounded delusional and psychotic.

"What were you doing fucking some other woman in the bed I bought you? You hadn't even had a chance to do me in it yet, and I catch you with some other tramp!"

"Tre, what you doing?" I hung the phone up.

"Ned, don't come sneaking around me like that," I whispered back.

I walked over to the couch and fell asleep, praying when I woke up it would be a new day, a better day.

Chapter Nineteen

Knock knock knock.

I jumped off the sofa, trying to get my bearings straight. The couch was not meant for sleeping long periods of time. My back ached with a vengeance. At least my stomach didn't hurt anymore. After reviewing the spot I slept in, I thanked God for the wisdom to put a towel down under me, especially once I saw the blood droplets. Mama would have tripped if I'd messed up her beloved sofa.

Knock knock knock.

What time was it anyway? The only person who'd normally come over here this time of morning had better not be standing outside my door. I went to mama's bedroom to check the time on her digital alarm clock. 10:30 AM. Our bedroom was empty, too. Ned's already up and out. Peeking outside the bedroom window was a fruitless exercise. I couldn't see anything. But I wouldn't move. I had a better chance of not being seen if I stayed in the room behind the curtain. I'm not certain how much time passed, but I finally caught a glimpse. He had the radio in his hand but not turned on. He ain't slick.

Before long he'd go home. It's too hot to stay outside. I closed the curtain.

Thirty minutes later the phone rang. While debating whether to answer, it stopped. Five minutes later it rang again.

"Hell-o?" I answered with attitude just in case the person on the other end wanted to start some shit.

"Why didn't you answer the door a minute ago?"

I didn't respond.

"Hello?"

"I'm here."

Minutes went by before either of us spoke.

"Fuck it. I'll let you go."

"Okay, whatever…" Click.

Once the sun went down some, I walked to the pool. Wearing my bathing suit top with a pair of cut-off denim shorts drew lots of sidebar comments. No one said a word until *after* I passed. Chicken heads too scared to talk that crap to my face. Their kids, too.

Locating a lounge chair opposite the heavy traffic area, I took a seat. The smell of chlorine plus the pool volleyball game in progress almost made me say 'to hell with my period'. But it would not be cute if I peed in the pool and traces of blood showed up in it. Can't hide red.

"Trekela, what happened to you yesterday?" It was Ms. Denise, standing there in white shorts and a t-shirt that read, *'Jesus - the option with present and future rewards'*. With one hand on her hip, she tried to frown, but her smile dominated instead.

"Hi Ms. Denise," I said, not wanting to look her in the eyes.

"I missed you," she said tenderly, almost whispering. I looked away.

"I need you to do something for me." She squatted next to me. She's probably heard about all the bad stuff I've been doing and wants to tell me to cut it out. Like the grown people who talk about me behind my back, she'll most likely tell me I'm on the road to being a teenage mother. But I was in no mood to hear that.

"The reason I came over was because I need you to serve as my helper this evening."

"Your helper? How?" I perked up, but still felt so unworthy.

"The apartment management approved my Jesus at the Clubhouse program. I came by your house to tell you. Didn't Ned give you my message?

"No, ma'am."

"That boy! I'm gonna get him when I see him. Next time I'll try to talk to your mother. Anyway, you can help me in a lot of ways. I need help facilitating the games, administering the craft time for the kids. I need help with the overhead projector during our praise and worship time. I need help serving snacks at the end of the night."

Wow! Can I do all that?

"Will you help me, Trekela? Please, please, please?"

I couldn't resist smiling at her antics. Of all the other kids, she came to me. I refused to let her down again.

"Okay. I'll help you."

"Yea!" she said clapping her hands, grinning ear to ear.

She gets way too excited about stuff. I had no problem

problem helping her. In fact, it's been a long time since I've been this excited about anything. But I have one burning question that I can't let go of. I feel silly even asking it. But more people have had trouble with this one issue regarding church or church-type activities.

"Ms. Denise?"

"Yes, sweetie."

"Do I have to wear a dress?"

Ms. Denise played my studio audience now. She laughed so hard her eyes watered. I thought it was a serious question.

She finally settled down. After wiping her eyes, she cleared her throat and regained her composure.

"Trekela, baby, wear whatever you feel comfortable in. God *ain't* looking at the outside, so neither will I," she said, giving my nose her signature pinch.

I really like her. And I'm excited about Jesus at the Clubhouse tonight. I still had no clue about what to wear. So, I decided to dress like Ms. Denise - shorts and a t-shirt. That way, I'd distinguish myself as her helper.

I ran home to change.

"Take that – unh!" David threw the ball at Anjanette, barely missing her head.

"All right, David. Don't make me suspend your throwing privileges," Ms. Denise warned.

"Heads up!" Walter threw it back. "Out!" he shouted to Michael, who's hit to the back sounded off. He retreated to the sideline walking like he wasn't hurt.

That's how each meeting started off. Two games of dodgeball, followed by two games illustrating bible principles. My favorite one required you to break into two teams, blind-fold a volunteer then try to decide which team is leading you in the way you're suppose to go. The other team attempts to get the blindfolded person to fall into a pit or something so they can laugh at him or her.

"Okay, troops, let's reassemble back in the clubhouse for our weekly talk."

"Please can we play one more game, Ms. Denise?"

"Yea, Ms. Denise, just one, pretty please?"

"Nope nope, we're through with games for the day. Let's go spend just a few minutes talking about the Lord." She grabbed Michael in a playful chokehold and led him by the neck into the clubhouse.

"Have a seat, quickly." They filed in and took a seat on the floor, quieting themselves down anticipating Ms. Denise's talk. I was curious to see what she'd say that could get them to behave so well.

"All-right. I need five volunteers…"

"Oooh, pick me, pick me."

"I wanna do it."

"Look over here."

"Hold on, hold on, y'all don't even know what I need volunteers for." She laughed and backed up as upright arms with wiggly hands at the end of them fought for her attention. When the hands and arms weren't enough, upright, bouncing bodies joined in.

"Back up, everyone, or no one will get picked. I won't pick anyone who's not seated." With that, everyone took a seat, but kept their arms in the air.

"Trekela, why don't you pick my volunteers for me." Instantly, all pleading glances focused on me to grant them their golden opportunity.

"She won't pick anyone who's not seated."

"Please, Trekela, please."

"Okay, I pick him, him, her, him and her," I said as I walked through the crowd physically tugging on the arms of my chosen ones.

"I knew she was gon' pick her brother," said an anonymous voice of one of the unlucky ones.

"That's what she suppose to do," said another unlucky one who understood why I picked my brother.

"All right, now. I'm giving each of you a calculator, okay? When I call out a number and tell you to perform a mathematical function on the calculator, I want all of you to do that to see if we get the same answer, okay? Do you understand?"

"What's a mathematical function?" asked one of my chosen ones, who I wanted to unchoose for asking such a dumb question. Apparently, others agreed since they snickered in the background.

"When I call out a number, I'll say add or subtract or multiply or divide. And that's all you have to do. Got it? See, it's not that hard." She is so great with these kids.
"Is everyone ready? What is $234 + 100$?"

The chosen ones vigorously punch numbers on the calculator, trying to be the first ones to get the answer.

"334!" Ned yelled out.

"Very good, Ned. Did anyone get another answer? No?" Looking around to verify, she continued, "Try 334 – 200?" Once again they pecked away at the electronic math whizzes in their hand.

"134!" Angie and Kayla said together.

"Excellent! Now, what is 334 +134?"

It took a few seconds longer for them to get the answer. Finally we hear, "468!"

"468? Is that what you got? Are you sure that's the right answer? Try it again."

With less rush and more precision, they recheck their calculations, this time checking with each other to see if they got the right answer.

Ned speaks up for the group. "Ms. Denise, we all got 468 again."

"Hmmm. That's strange. Let me recheck my math...oh my goodness, wait a minute. I see what happened here. Does everyone see this button on the calculator?" She held up the calculator and pointed to the "M" button. "Do you know what this button does? It allows you to hold in memory certain numbers or answers to problems. All you have to do to record an answer, right or wrong, is to push this button, and *Voila* there it is. The problem with storing numbers is it can throw off new calculations you're trying to run. But check this out. PING! See that? It's gone. No more numbers left in the memory. No more errors in my calculation. Now, let me run the same calculation again. Lets see…334 + 134 = 468.

"Just as I erased my errors from my calculator, God said He'd erase my errors called sin from my life. Isaiah 43:25 says this, 'I, I am the One who forgives all your sins, for my sake; I will not remember your sins.' Remember that memory button that recorded my mathematical mistakes?"

"Yes!"

"Well, God said He's not like that. He doesn't want to keep a record of our mistakes. Instead, PING! He erases them and doesn't remember them anymore. When God sent His son Jesus to die for us, because of His death and resurrection, when we choose Him, all our sins are forgiven. So when we do wrong things, let's not try to hide them. Rather, let's commit to take them to God in prayer and apologize to Him for them and allow Him to PING! erase them. Everybody say PING!"

"PING!" we sang in unison.

"Father, thank You for each one of these precious lives that sit here in Your presence. Help them to remember this week that You're not trying to disqualify them because of their sin. You gave us Jesus who is the reason we can come directly to You asking for forgiveness. Thank You that we don't have to hide our sins from You, but can come to You in prayer asking for forgiveness and PING! You erase them. Amen."

I tried to wipe my eyes before anyone saw me.

"All right, who wants to pray our closing prayer?"

"Ooh, Ms. Denise, pick me, pick me!"

"I wanna pray today!"

"You always get to pray. Let somebody else have a turn."

"Ms. Denise, I haven't prayed yet. Please?"

"Wow! I'm so glad to see all of you enthusiastic prayer warriors. Let's see...ah...how about...Dee Dee!"

"Ah, man. Why she get to pray?"

"I want to encourage y'all to keep up the excitement about praying. But don't think you can only pray when you attend Jesus at the Clubhouse. God is everywhere. He likes it when you talk to Him. So, make a commitment this week to spend time talking to God in prayer, okay?"

"Yes, ma'am," they responded together.

"Okay...Dee Dee..." she said nodding to her to begin the prayer. Turning to everyone else she commanded, "Heads down, eyes closed. This is not a time to play, okay?"

All around the room, kids bowed their heads and closed their eyes waiting on Dee Dee to pray. Even Early, who's known for always acting up, bowed obediently.

Popping her lips between pauses, Dee Dee prayed, "Dear God...thank You for this day...thank You for Ms. Denise and her teaching us about You...help us to remember that You not keeping a negative record and we should ask You for forgiveness of our sins and...and...that's it...love Dee Dee...I mean, amen."

"Amen," we said in unison.

"A-men," Ms. Denise said flipping Dee Dee the thumbs up sign and winking. "Let's see, I need everyone to line up for snacks. Ladies first, gentleman." The boys scrunched back barely allowing enough room for the girls to squeeze in front of them.

"Trekela, be sure everyone gets two cookies and one

177

cup of juice." Turning to the group she said, "No seconds."

"Ahhh, Ms. Denise," they said collectively.

Once everyone left, I stayed behind to help clean up.

"Trekela, I want to thank you for helping me tonight. I really appreciate it."

"You're welcome, Ms. Denise. I had fun."

"Can I ask you something?" No smiles, no laughter. She didn't flinch. Just kept throwing cups away and picking up the big pieces of cookie that had fallen on the floor. Here it comes. I knew she was too good to be true.

"Would you like to go to Astroworld this weekend?"

I could hardly contain my excitement. "Yes, ma'am!"

"My church is taking a group of kids from our youth department. You're the only one I'm inviting from here, so it hush-hush, okay?"

"Okay."

"Now this invitation is tentative. We first have to ask your mother."

Damn. I mean, dang.

"Is she home right now?"

"She should be. I mean, unless she went to happy hour after work."

"Mmm. Okay, well if she's not home tonight, I'll make a special trip over here tomorrow to see her. Or maybe she and I can talk on the phone. This is my way of letting you know how special you are to me and thanking you for being such a big help to me."

"Yes, ma'am." Even if I don't get to go, like celebrities say after the awards show, it was nice just being nominated.

Chapter Twenty

"Hey, Ms. Denise!" The kids in the square who'd just spent two hours with her still hadn't got enough of her. She enjoyed 'queen status'. All at once they crowded around. As she covered *me* with her left arm, everyone else battled for the remaining arm, while still others tried to capture her attention singing praise songs she taught.

"Jesus is worthy of the highest praise...of the highest praise...Jesus is wor-r-thy, Jesus is worthy of the highest praise...He's worthy of the hi-igh-est praise," one began 'til everyone joined in, including Ms. Denise. When she started to sing, so did I. They walked with us all the way to my front porch, singing and carrying on.

"Hey my pumpkins!" she said holding her hands to signal our entourage to be silent for an announcement. "Tre and I have business to tend to, okay? We're going in to talk to her mother about something. I need for you to continue singing if you want, but give us some privacy. Is that fair? Can you help me out?"

Silence was followed my soft mumbling and secret whispers. "Ooh, what she in trouble for now?"

179

Ignoring them, I said, "Ms. Denise, let me walk in first to make sure she's dressed. I'll be right back."

Luckily, mama was home, although she didn't look real good. I walked in on her talking on the phone in her bedroom.

"Girl, my children needed stuff, but instead I furnished his raggedy little apartment out of the goodness of my heart…no, he didn't ask me to do it…I know…I just feel like such a fool." Her voice cracked and quivered so much I could barely understand her.

"Mama." She turned around.

"Hold on a minute." Cupping the mouthpiece of the phone, "Tre, how long have you been standing there? What have I told you about entering my room without knocking?"

"I did knock. Ms. Denise is outside and she wants to talk to you."

"Let me call you back…I'll be okay…just pray for me…all right then…bye bye."

I went back to the front door. "You can come in, Ms. Denise. Mama is putting on some clothes."

"Thanks, Trekela." She turned back to the crowd and placed her index finger over her mouth as she walked slowly into our apartment closing the door behind her. "Man, y'all have a beautiful home. You're truly blessed."

Ms. Denise continued to survey our apartment offering silent approval with her head nods and cemented smile.

Mama walked in. "Ms. Denise, this is my mama, Ann Baden." While mama had at least run a comb through her hair, that did nothing to disguise her red, puffy eyes.

"Ms. Baden, it's so nice to meet you. How are you?"

"I've had better days. It's good to meet you, too. My children are crazy about you, especially Ned. After Vacation Bible School, he wouldn't stop singing the songs you taught them. You're doing a great work." She sniffled.

"Well, thank you. I love your children, too. And Ned is a great kid. But Trekela is my special angel."

"Really?" Mama asked almost in disbelief.

"Oh yes ma'am. I've recruited her to help me with a new program the apartment management has approved for me to do. It's a lot like VBS, except we call it Jesus at the Clubhouse."

"I like that. How often will you meet?"

"Right now I'm thinking we'll meet a couple times each week. Because I'm in school right now, I'm trying to work the program around my class schedule."

"Okay. But let me know if you have any trouble out of Trekela. She's 11 going on 21. I have to watch her," she said like having to care for me makes life bitter for her.

"Who...Trekela?"

"Unh-huh. So be careful, honey."

"I can't believe that." Pulling me towards her and wrapping me in her arms she added, "when I first met Trekela, I knew there was something special about her. She reminded me so much of myself at her age. I don't believe God makes mistakes in anything He creates. Trekela bears the very image of God, and I want her to believe that, to value that. I'm trying to teach the kids around here that God created them for a reason and the only way to truly live out what God had in mind for them from the beginning is for them to consider a relationship with Him through Jesus."

Mama said nothing, just continued listening.

"I know it may seem to some Trekela is growing up kinda fast."

"You can say that again."

"But I believe there is more to her than meets the eye. She really does have a beautiful heart. Every time I talk to her she's mannerable, always saying yes ma'am and all that. I really believe God has an awesome plan for her life. But to experience God's best, she needs to learn obedience."

"Obedience is definitely not one of her strong points."

"It's not always one of my strong points either." Ms. Denise laughed. "I believe God allowed me to meet her for a reason. And if it's okay with you, I'd appreciate the chance to spend more time with her, starting this weekend. My church is taking some of the kids from our church to Astroworld and I want Trekela to come as my special guest."

"Well, I don't really have any extra money for that right now."

"Oh, no, I'd pay for everything."

"I don't know. Trekela doesn't really deserve a trip to Astroworld."

"Mama, what have I done?" *that you know about, that is.* "Why can't I get away from here?" I asked, tears streaming down my face.

"Um…Ms. Baden, can I talk to you alone?"

"Trekela, go to your room."

From the bedroom, I could hear conversation, but not make out any of the words. Whether or not mama said I could go didn't matter. I planned to be on that church bus on Saturday.

First she wouldn't let me go swimming with my
friends. Now this. Outside my window I heard Blowfly. No
need to peek out. And what did she mean Ned loved Ms.
Denise more than me? I loved her more than anybody around
here. She's always in my corner. I have feelings, too, but no
one considers that. It hurt to know everyone thought one thing
about me, when the direct opposite of what they believe about
me was actually true. All they had to do was spend time with
me, which no one ever had.

I went back to the door and cracked it open.

"…maybe if you let her spend some time away from
here…give her a chance to meet some kids from the
church…you might see a change for the better."

I closed the door and cried.

Saturday morning I met Ms. Denise at the front office.

The church van, practically filled to capacity, parked
next to the curb by the mailbox. Walking up, the scene on the
bus sounded out of control. Kids laughed and screamed to the
top of their lungs in amusement. If I'd known the bus would
arrive early, I would have gotten here before them. I hated the
idea of them watching me walk up. At first they didn't see me.
Then everything got quiet. They saw me then. Ms. Denise met
me before I arrived to the van.

"Good morning, Sunshine."

"Good morning."

"You all set to have some fun today?"

"Yes, ma'am."

Sliding the van door back, she introduced me to the other kids. "Everyone, I'd like you to meet Trekela. Trekela, starting from the front row, that's Jasper, Angie, and Dara. Then we have Rashika, Tangela, Corey and Brian. Holding up the back row…who's ducking back there? David, quit play-ing." Everyone laughed. "Finally, we have David and Eisha."

"Hi. Nice to meet you." No one said anything.

"Hey…what about me?"

"Sorry, Diane. Trekela, the lady sitting up front behind the driver's wheel is Ms. Diane. She is the one responsible for transporting this van full of precious cargo."

"Welcome, Trekela."

"Thanks." I wish Robin or somebody could have come with me.

"Jasper, why don't you move to the back and let Trekela sit up front?"

"I'll go to the back," Angie said.

"No, I will," Dara insisted as she dashed to the back of the van. Everyone else snickered.

"All right, now. Settle down." Ms. Denise gave Dara a look that needed no words. I hope she got the point.

I took a seat on the front row next to the door and behind Ms. Denise. Ms. Diane and she talked back and forth about…I don't know…grown people stuff.

"Trekela, I like yo' short set. You must plan to be on Soul Train or somethin'," David said, commenting on my new black fitted t-shirt with silvery-metallic butterfly image on the front and matching black shorts. The other kids snickered at his remark.

184

Either Ms. Denise didn't hear or she felt like she didn't need to get involved. So, I took care of it.

"Yea, I've been rehearsing my steps wit' yo mama. Is she meeting us at Astroworld, or will we need to pick her up from her corner? Will your daddy be mad if she don't bring home money tonight?"

"Ooh..." Everyone fell silent. Ms. Denise turned around. I'd hoped she hadn't heard me, like she supposedly didn't hear David.

"What's going on?" She waited for someone to answer. When no one did, she asked me specifically. "Trekela?"

Since no one else said anything, neither would I.

"Okay, that's the last time I want to hear that kind of talk from any of you." She addressed the whole van, but everyone knew she really meant me. When she faced front again, I turned back to look at David and the rest of them.

As long as we understand each other...

At Astroworld, I stuck to Ms. Denise like spandex to a black woman's anatomy.

"Do you wanna ride anything?"

"No, ma'am. I don't like the way rollercoasters make my stomach feel."

"Me, too. The last time I got on one, I threw up all over everybody in my section."

I'm definitely not riding now.

"It's hot as the devil out here. You want something to drink?"

"Yes, ma'am. It's hot as hel-...uh, my throat is dry."

I looked towards Ms. Denise to see if she caught my slip-up. She didn't flinch.

"Sir, can we get two Cokes please?"

"Would you care to purchase them in souvenir glasses for $1.95?" the cashier asked.

"Yea…okay. Can we get some cotton candy, too?" Ms. Denise said.

We took a seat at a table under a tree by one of Astroworld's many fountains. I love it out here. Nightfall wouldn't come soon enough for me. First I needed a break from the heat. Second, I get to see up close the nightly fireworks show. Sometimes we caught it from the Village. But it's not the same.

"Trekela, are you having fun?"

"Yes, ma'am." *But not because I'm at Astroworld.* I took a few seconds to muster the courage to make my next statement. No matter how I said it, I'd still sound hokey. "Thank you for spending time with me."

She smiled. "You know how I told your mom that you remind me of myself at your age?"

"Unh-huh."

"Well, just like you appear to be, I didn't have a lot of friends, except for boys. And I grew up in an apartment complex where everybody seemed to be in your business. They'd criticize me and make me feel awful about myself."

"What happened to change you?" She always seemed happy go lucky. I never would have thought.

"I made a choice to follow Jesus."

"That's it?"

"That was the first step. After I made that choice, things didn't change right away. I still had few if any girlfriends. My little boyfriends, most of whom were like brothers to me, still hung around. People still talked bad about me. But I was determined to live the life my Creator destined me to live."

Angie, Dara, Rashika, Tangela and Eisha walked by with Ms. Diane. "Hey, Ms. Denise!" they shouted out. Never mind that I sat right next to her and no one spoke to me. They really looked goofy wearing skirts and dresses with tennis shoes.

"How'd you do it?"

"Do what?"

"Follow through on your determination?"

"First, I started going to church. There was a lady who'd come to pick me up and take me.

Sis. Lightner.

"A lot of times, I didn't have a clue what the preacher meant in his sermons. But she made herself available to answer any questions I had about God after church.

"The key, Trekela," she said holding up her index finger, "is accepting Jesus Christ into your heart as your personal Savior. God never refuses a relationship with His creation. If you want to know Him, He's not trying to disqualify you.

"Before I knew it, I listened, believed and acted on what I heard. I willingly submitted to the influences of one environment over the other. My setting didn't change, but my heart and mind did." She spoke with so much passion.

187

"Do me a favor and look at the lives of the people around you? Is anyone living like you hope to live? Do any of them make good choices and receive good results that you want for your life? Just look around. You're a smart girl. You recognize raggediness when you see it, don't you?"

I nodded.

"Make a daily decision to not be one of them. Decide once and for all you want the very best God has for your life. And be clear you won't experience His best for you living any kind of way.

"Right now, think of one person in your life who you hope to be like. You got that person in your mind?"

Yea...Ms. Denise.

"*Do* what you see that person do. Think of another person in your life who you definitely don't want to be like."

The list is endless.

"*Don't* do what you see that person do."

If I'm like her as a young person, I hope I'm still like her when I get older.

"Trekela, I want you to know that I love you and I'm here for you if you need anything." She grabbed my hand and squeezed it.

I smiled, nodded and dabbed the corners of my eyes to keep tears from falling.

Chapter Twenty-one

When I walked in the house, Ned greeted me at the door smiling ear to ear.

"Hey, Tre. What you bring me?" I thought he'd be upset because he couldn't go with me.

"Here." I handed him a left-over bag of taffy.

"Hey mama!" I said as I walked towards the sounds of clanging pots in the kitchen. At the doorway, I stopped cold.

"Hey, boo!" mama said. Her eyes were bright and happy. She decorated her lips fire engine red and dressed her ears with big, gold hoops.

"What'sup lil mama? How was Astroworld?"

"Hey Chester. Fine."

"I've been tryin' ta tell yo' mama me, her, you and Ned oughta go out there before the summer is over."

Mama looked him up and down and smiled. Chester walked behind her and pulled her front to his.

As they walked back to her bedroom, Chester said, "Why don' y'all go outside for a while?"

"It's dark out there," I said.

"Just don't leave the square. Y'all a be ah-ight." They disappeared.

"Trekela…come here for a minute?"

Darrel looked high. I think he was a senior at Worthing or Sterling High School. Ms. Pat and he usually hung out on her porch. Tonight they sat on fold up chairs under his bridgeway. Before heading in my direction, he leaned over to Ms. Pat and said something. She laughed as he twitched his way over to me.

"Girl, where you been all day?"

"Astroworld."

"Ummm. Did you *enjoy* yourself?"

"Yea."

"Oh. Why come you ain't talkin' to me in full sentences?"

"Tired," I said covering my mouth while I yawned.

"Look, I've been checking you out lately. Somethin' seem different about you."

I heard after you get your period your womanly traits developed.

"Yea."

"Where yo' boyfriend RJ at?"

"In his skin."

"Ah-ight. I'ma dismiss yo' smart-alek comments tonight since you lookin' so good. But check this out," leaning closer towards me, "I don't mean to get in yo' bizness or nothin' but you know he got another girlfriend over in Orleans, huh?"

"Who's the first girlfriend?

"What?"

"I said who's the first girlfriend that would make the other young lady 'the other girlfriend'?"

"Ooh. Well I guess she's the only one then. But speaking of girlfriends, you know I've been lookin' for one, right?"

What?!

"Yea I've been checking you out. I think you got a chance to hold that spot," he said looking at me for a reaction.

Where's the Pepto Bismol when you need it?

I didn't think he liked females. I've never seen him with one. Rather than address his sexual partner choice, which obviously was female since he's sitting here trying to holla' at me, I came at him from another angle, one that I was sure would cripple his advances.

"I'm too young for you."

"Age don' matta. Besides, girls mature fasta' than boys. So we'd be perfect together."

I must admit, I slightly enjoyed him begging me for what I knew he'd never get. Nevertheless, I was more disgusted than flattered. The very sound of his voice made my flesh crawl.

Walking out our apartment zipping his pants and looking satisfied, Chester called out. "Tre and Ned, yo' mama said it's time to come in the house."

Thank God.

"Where you going, Chester?" Ned asked.

To hell I hope.

"Gotta go make that money, man. Y'all get in the house."

As I lifted from the stairs, my flip flop fell off my foot. Darrel caught it. "At least I got to hold somethin' of yours tonight."

Mama was in the shower when we came in and couldn't hear the phone ringing.

"Hello?"

"Yes...is Ann home?"

"Yes she is. May I ask who's calling?"

"Would you tell her Mr. Tolbert is holding for her."

"She can't come to the phone right now."

"Ah, young lady, if you'd just do as I've asked I'm sure she'd be more than happy to stop what she's doing and come to the phone. Now, please let your mother know I'm holding. Thank you."

WHAP! I slammed the mouthpiece of the receiver down on the countertop hoping the sound was loud enough to bust *Mr. Tolbert's* eardrum.

Standing outside the bathroom, I called to mama. "Mama, some man named Mr. Tolbert is on the phone for you. He *told* me to *tell* you he's holding for you."

"I'll take the call in my bedroom."

I walked back to the kitchen. "I got it, Tre. You can hang the phone up now...Hey, boo. I was hoping you'd call me."

She sounded like a prostitute. I couldn't stand it.

Chapter Twenty-two

Ms. Denise invited me to the Houston Public Library's "Griot Series" on the courtyard of their new building downtown. I dressed in my new white Astroworld t-shirt Ms. Denise bought me. Since the shirt hung long, it looked as if I didn't have anything on underneath. The sun beat us down. We didn't mind too much though. We were too captivated by the Griot's stories of talking animals. His voice characterizations sounded exactly as I pictured a lion or a bear would sound if they could talk.

I couldn't wait to get home to tell mama about the Griot.

When I got home, I found her bedroom door cracked with her laying on her side talking on the phone. By the way she was talking I knew it was a man.

"I had a good time last night, too, Leon…yea, we need to get together real soon…"

I closed the door all the way, certain she'd want to keep this conversation between her and _Leon_ private, whoever he was.

Ms. Denise's church sponsored Gospel Skate Night every Wednesday at Super Skate. They'd invite other church youth groups to take part.

As I sat down to put on my skates I thought I heard someone call my name. After looking around and not seeing anyone, I continued to lace up my skates. I skated around the rink a few times. It was difficult trying to groove to Shirley Caesar on skates. Now if they played Confunkshun, I could do what I do. But no such thing will happen in here tonight.

We competed against other youth groups in skating competitions – skating relay, skating techniques, tricks on skates, etc. Whenever there was a white youth group that would participate, they'd always win the 'tricks on skates' part of the competition. Without fail, they'd always have someone who could turn flips. I usually won the relay for Ms. Denise's church. Only after that did Dara and them have anything to do with me.

"All right Trekela!"

"Way to go, Trekela!"

"Trekela, sit by me on the bus."

Loading the bus, I heard someone calling my name again. I looked back.

Oh my God. "Mary!"

"Hey, Trekela!" She hugged me tight around my neck, giggling the whole time.

"Hey, Mary! I'm so happy to see you!"

"Trekela, you look beautiful."

"I feel sweaty in these jeans. But they did help to protect my knees."

"Protect them from what?" she asked. "You're a good skater."

"Who are you hear with?"

"My friends from church. Mama's here, too. Come say hi to her."

I went numb for a second and tried to figure out a way out of it.

"I don't want the bus to leave me. Tell her hi for me."

"Okay. I betta go, too, before I get left. Give me a hug. It's good to see you going and growing in the Lord."

Is that what I'm doing?

"It's good to see you, too, Mary." We embraced again. As we let go, she could tell I wanted to ask her about them.

Reading my mind, "Nae and Mimi aren't doing as good as you. They're with their daddy's mama in Brazoria. Pray for 'em when you think about 'em." Her mood sobered when she talked about her sisters. I wished I hadn't pressed the issue, indirectly anyway.

Ms. Denise dropped me off at the front office. Before I got out the van, she asked, "Trekela, how would you like to go to church with me this Sunday? I can come pick you up by 9:00 AM for Sunday School?"

"Yea, Trekela. You'll be in our class," Rashika said. The others chimed in with similar comments.

It had been a long time since I'd been to church. I wondered if I could still fit some of the dresses in my closet.

"I tell you what. After church, you and I can go hang out for a minute. How 'bout that?"

I loved spending time with Ms. Denise. Maybe church would be good for me.

"Ned, is mama in the house?"

"Yea, but she got company."

"Who's she with *now*?" I asked exasperated. Ned's friends stopped what they were doing. It was too late to take the comment back.

"Mr. Allen."

"Who?"

"Mr. Allen."

"Where she know him from?"

"TRE, I DON'T KNOW. GO ASK HER YOUR- SELF!"

When I walked in the house, the record player was on, but the living room was empty. I peeked down the hallway and saw her bedroom door closed.

Early the next morning, before the sun came up, I heard voices at the front door. At the window, I saw a man walking backwards, blowing kisses towards our door. Mama must have still been standing there. He was one of many. When the door closed, I jumped back in bed. I heard mama go to the bath- room and turn on the shower.

I had a hard time adjusting to all those men in and out of mama's bedroom. It was only a matter of time before it caught up with her. Nothing escapes these nosy folks around here.

I'll never forget being embarrassed when one of Ned's little friends said, "Yo' mama sure got a lot of *'friends'*."

We knew what he meant. No one has ever seen mama with female friends.

One time, I went with mama to one of her girlfriend's house. The more wine they sipped, the looser their lips became.

"Girl, I don't know what to say for these old sorry ass men. As far as I'm concerned, they can only do one thing for me."

"…and if they don't do *that* right the first time around, you move on," mama's friend added.

"You know I really loved Chester and only wanted to be with him. But he showed me how he felt about me."

"Ann, you can't trust none of 'em. And if the nigga' ain't decorating your finger with a little sumpin' sumpin' to signal a commitment, he don't own you. Shit, I say go for all the scrum you can handle."

Mama held her glass up. "Here's to a lifetime supply of scrum…however you can get it!"

"Cheers!"

Giggling, they clicked glasses.

"I've tried to do it the right way. What do I have to show for it? Memories of getting my ass kicked by the man I was supposed to spend the rest of my life with, and $2,000 of debt to Foley's thanks to the only man I trusted my heart to after my divorce.

"I'm sick of trying. If they want to screw without discernment, so will I."

As we backed down the driveway heading home, mama yelled out, "Speaking of scrum, tell your brother Dexter the

the next time I see him, I wanna catch him with his draws down."

I looked up from the backseat not believing what I'd just heard.

"Lord, I forgot my child was back there," she laughed, partly amused and partly embarrassed that my thoughts of her were now confirmed.

My mama's a ho.

One week later, she got what she wanted, but not without all of us paying a heavy price.

Chapter Twenty-three

It was Saturday, the fourth of July morning. Nothing moved in the square. Everyone rested from the Friday night partying. Around holidays, folks in the square go crazy. Darrel put his speaker outside and threw a spur of the moment square party. Since mama went to the club Friday night, Ned and I got to stay outside late with everyone else. Being Ms. Denise's helper at Jesus at the Clubhouse has increased my popularity with some of the girls in my square again. Instead of talking about me, now their mamas all talk about my mama. I hated them for talking negative about my mama. But I didn't con-cern myself with it too much. If push comes to shove, at least mama can cuss them out.

Everything was real cool Friday night. Then came Saturday morning.

I woke up to noises coming from mama's bedroom. After stretching, I hopped off the top bunk, went to the living room to put on my Kool and the Gang album hoping to drown them out. "Celebration" was my jam. There was a knock at the door. Who would be coming to our house this time of of morning? I peeked out the curtain and snickered. I opened the door. She's busted.

"Hey Chester."

"Hey lil' bit. Where's ya' mama?"

"She's in her bedroom."

He smiled, patted me on the head and headed back to mama's bedroom, the area he knew so well. I turned my music down a bit to hear the action going on in the back, but still loud enough to hear JT's sweet voice. I kept waiting to hear something. But nothing came.

All of sudden mama appeared, fully dressed. She had a strange look on her face, like she wanted me to feel it wasn't a big deal and everything was okay. But I could tell everything wasn't okay. Suddenly this situation was no longer funny. Fear and panic gripped my insides. Chester followed mama very closely, refusing to look at me. He closed the door behind him as they went outside. Thirty seconds later I heard my mama scream out.

"CHESTER, I'M SORRY!#&!

I couldn't believe it. I know that motherfucker didn't hit my mama! I ran to the bedroom to wake Ned.

"Ned, Ned, wake up. Chester is beating mama!" All of a sudden, Ned jumped out of bed and he and I were united in fear. We ran out the house but didn't see mama.

"CHESTER,...NOOO!!!" We looked towards the parking lot beyond the washateria and there was mama and Chester walking towards the square struggling over a shotgun. Chester headed towards our apartment with mama walking backwards trying to stop him from getting to our apartment to shoot the man in her bed.

But what if he decided to shoot mama instead?

Screaming and crying, Ned and I ran upstairs to Ms. Sheila's apartment. Once we arrived at the top of the steps, I noticed someone peering behind Ms. Pat's curtains. When I glanced over there, the curtains quickly closed. Frantic, we banged on the door. I begged God, *"Please Lord...please Lord...please Lord..."* I knew He understood what I needed from Him. Ms. Sheila eventually opened the door and pulled Ned and I to safety. However, we cried so hard she had a difficult time discerning our words.

"Mama...Chester...fight...gun..." was all we could say as Ms. Sheila took Ned in her arms and Darlene, Ms. Sheila's baby sister from Louisiana, buried my face in her chest, giving us comfort and temporary security.

Then, the shotgun went off. Mama screamed.

"Oh, God", Ms. Sheila gasped.

"MAMA!!!", Ned screamed.

My heart stopped. Darlene went to the window to see what happened.

"Chester...please stop", mama sobbed. We relaxed somewhat at the sound of mama's voice, but were still on edge for the drama still in full effect.

"Man, get ya' ass outside!", Chester hollered while trying to kick in the front door of our apartment. Mama's friend had barricaded himself on the inside.

"Come on...brang ya' ass outside and stop hidin' behind the door like a punk!"

"Dexter, stay inside please. Don't come out or you'll make the situation worse," mama pleaded.

"What the fuck you tryin' to protect that nigga fo', huh? Huh, bitch?" WHAP!

"Ugh-huh!" mama cried. "Chester, I'm sorry. Please don't do this."

"Wait a minute. I got somethin' for yo' ass. Hold on," he said. Chester walked back to his truck.

We saw mama's friend make a speedy escape, wearing only the sheets from her bed. Chester walked back to the apartment looking for the man. A couple of people stood around outside on their porches in housecoats watching this debacle, not offering any assistance. No one bothered to even do so much as call the police.

Me, mama and Ned followed behind begging him to stop. Frustrated that the bedroom was now empty, he turned to mama. As he cussed her out, he reached for her purse and took out her wallet.

"Yea, bitch, since you got some other nigga' paying' yo' way, you won't need this cash, will you? Unh-huh…how…how 'bout these credit cards, too?…Yea, and uh, how you gon' drive out to the country without yo' drivers license? You know those redneck faggot deputies down there don't give a shit about haulin' yo' black ass off to jail for somethin' as simple as drivin' wit' no license, right, bitch?"

He helped himself to everything in her wallet. He then knocked over her jewelry box and perfume bottles on her dresser and walked out the apartment, I prayed for the last time.

Mama locked the door and stood with her back against it for a minute.

She composed herself, wiped her face and smiled. "Ned...Tre...shhh...shhh...shhh...come on now. Everything's okay now." She wrapped one arm around Ned and the other around me.

"Stop crying, okay? Hey, hey, listen to me...shh, listen. I'm okay and you're okay. It's all over with now. He's gone."

"Yea, but... for... how... long? What... if he... comes back... to... kill... you?" Ned asked in between hiccups. The thought of being without mama was more than he could stand. He cried harder.

We were still afraid. Yet the tears we cried were no longer tears of fear. They were tears of anguish and gut-wrenching pain over all that had transpired and what almost was.

"Hey, hey, be quiet. He won't come back. I won't let him. It's over now and we're okay", mama said in a sweet voice, shifting her head from right to left to talk to both of us. She smiled as she stroked my forehead.

"Everything's okay. Stop crying. It's okay now."

But we continued crying, wanting to feel secure again. And the look in mama's eyes wasn't enough to reassure us. In a thousand lifetimes, no one could have convinced us we'd be part of this kind of drama. It really didn't matter what she said. We wouldn't be easily comforted.

"Tre...Ned...stop crying. *C'mon, let's get dressed and go hang out at Aunt Sis'...*", she pleaded. Finally she succumbed to our brokenness. We all wept bitterly over our choices, especially mama and me.

Eventually, we calmed down long enough to bathe and get dressed to "celebrate" the fourth of July. With broken hearts and wounded spirits, we braved the rest of the day.

To the God I only seem to call on when I want something... thank you.

Chapter Twenty-four

"Hey, boo! Hey, man!" Aunt Sis pulled us into her.

"Hey, Auntie."

"Hey, Aunt Sis'."

"Tre, uh, that's an interesting outfit. Ain't you gon' be hot?" Without waiting for my response, she continued, "Y'all ready to go to the beach?" Turning to mama, "Ann, I got coupons for Church's 20-piece mixed. And Weingarten's had a sale on sodas, so I picked some up for the holiday weekend."

"Why don't we just go to the park? Traveling I-45 on holidays is maddening. Herman Park is closer."

"Okay. The park is cool."

Once we arrived, I looked around trying to make sure Chester wasn't here. Even if he was though he'd be difficult to spot in this sea of black people, the likes of which I'd never seen concentrated in one location in all my life. Usually, I'd be excited about the prospects of meeting new people, boys that is. All I could think about was "what if Chester is here?" Ned and I tried to stay as close to mama as she'd let us. We wanted to protect her.

"Pooh bears, why don't y'all go swing? Let me and

Aunt Sis' sit here and talk about grown folks stuff. I'll watch you from here. Now, go play, okay?"

"Yes, ma'am."

Ned and I walked to the swing set closest to where they sat.

Four other kids occupied the swings ahead of us. Rather than search for another set we could get on right away but would take mama out of our immediate view, we decided to wait it out.

"Bobby, don't push me too high!" one of the little girls said to the man pushing her from behind.

"I'm not. Quit acting so scary," he chided.

Occasionally we glanced over at mama and Auntie to make sure mama was okay. Watching them laugh seemed to put Ned at ease. Mama wiped the corner of her eyes every once in a while. A large group gathered underneath the cov- ered area decorated with balloons and banners singing happy birthday. We enjoyed the dog and frisbee tricks, courtesy of the only white person in the whole park. Love 94 must have barred the rest of them. For most of the day, we swung in full view of mama and Auntie. I think Ned wanted to venture over to the seesaw and monkey bars, but wouldn't go without me. And I wouldn't let mama out of my sight.

I swung so long that when I got off, my legs wobbled as I struggled to regain balance.

Ned laughed. "Tre, you look funny!"

Trees hid the sun during the late afternoon hours pro- viding some relief from the heat. The later it got, the better it felt outside. The better I felt. Ned pointed to the black stain left on my gouchos.

"Man, this stain probably won't come out."

"Good. Now you can throw those ugly thangs away," Ned said before he took off running. I chased him in a circle.

"Tre...Ned?" Mama beckoned us back over to the sheet. "Time to go home."

Ned looked at me. My heart pounded. We trudged back to the car in silence.

"Did y'all have fun today?"

"Yes," we said in monotoned unison.

"We'll have to do this on a regular basis." Ned and I said nothing. "Maybe next time we can go to the zoo, too."

"Mama, Ms. Denise invited me to church with her tomorrow. I need a dress."

"Tre!" she said exasperated. "Why are you just now telling me you need a dress? You know I don't have..."

"I have some stuff I've been meanin' to see if she could fit at the house," Auntie abruptly interrupted.

"They ain't too grown for Tre, huh? Don't have my child looking like some floozy."

"Shoot, I don't know what you talkin' 'bout. All my clothes is classy." Before getting in the car, she tugged at her shorts in the crotch area.

I hope no one else saw that.

Both closets in her two-bedroom apartment were filled to capacity. The spare bedroom closet was where she kept the clothes she outgrew. While Auntie frantically pulled out dresses, mama sifted through them for ones she thought were "age-appropriate". I stood off to the side awaiting my chance to provide input.

With of all those dresses, mama only found three.

"Mama, those dresses look like they're in a time warp or somethin'."

"I know you didn't," Auntie said with attitude all over her face.

"Girl, I know you betta' get on over here and be grateful you even got these to choose from."

"If I don't have a choice, I guess I'll take all of them." Now I had an attitude.

I sat with Ned in the living room until it was time to go.

"Lord, help me with this child. Sis', let me have 'em all. I'll give you a little somethin' on them the next time I get paid."

"Don't worry about it. Let me show you this other dress I got on sale. Come on, it's in the other room."

Darkness fell hours before. Yet the square was still in full effect. Smoking pits, domino and card games, music blasting from every which way. Walking into this scene made me sort of wish we'd hung around here for the day. Then mama stopped dead in her tracks.

"Oh God!"

On our front door, someone diagonally spray painted "HO!". As we got closer, we noticed the front window broken. With one final defiant act, Chester vandalized the peace in our home for the last time. Ned and I each took one of mama's hands and walked towards our home, refusing to look at anyone. My vision blurred from all the tears my eyes held but refused to release.

"Don't cry," Ned said.

I looked over at Ned to reassure him I was okay. When he didn't return my gaze, I followed the direction of his eyes to mama. As I watched tears make tracks down her face, I could no longer hold mine.

She opened the door and turned on the lights. To our surprise, on the floor behind the curtain was a rock, a note and mama's drivers license and credit cards rubber banded together. Mama read the note, ignoring Ned and I standing next to her peeking over her shoulders.

"Her is your shiit bak. I dident want to hert Ned and Tree Keylo. I kept the $$$. You git payed nex weeke. So you can spair it."

Had he paid more attention in English class, we could have read this two-lined note faster.

Mama wiped her tears and smiled. "Tre, what time you want me to wake you for church?" Stroking my hair, she worked her fingers down to my roots. "Ooh, it's time for your retouch, huh? Go get the relaxer from under the sink."

I preferred for my hair to be permed by a professional. Seeing as I had no money, mama would do. As I walked forward to get the relaxer, mama's fingers were still in my hair. But before I left her reach, she pulled me back to her. For the first time in a long time, mama's arms lovingly wrapped around me.

"Tre...I'm so sorry," she whispered.

Unsure of what to say, I didn't say anything, just enjoyed being close to her. We embraced for several minutes.

When her silent apologies were exhausted, she let go.

"Don't forget the Vaseline to base your edges, and my gloves, okay?"

" 'kay. I love you, mama."

"Love you, too, Tre." She playfully pinched my nose and winked.

Chapter Twenty-five

I arrived at the clubhouse at 8:45 AM. What my homely dress lacked, my newly straightened hair made up for.

The church bus pulled up. I hated being the last stop for pick up. Fighting for a good seat got old.

"Hey Sweetie." Ms. Denise got off the bus to hug me. "You look beautiful."

"Hey Trekela!" Everyone seemed excited to see me.

"Come sit by us." Rashika patted the empty space next to her.

"Your hair looks gooood!" Angie said.

"Who did it?" Dara asked running her fingers through the curls.

"I didn't know your hair was this long."

I enjoyed the attention, but didn't like people touching my hair.

Sunday School was nothing like Jesus at the Clubhouse. The kids in church seemed more out of control in class than the kids in the square. I expected more from them. Our teacher spent more time chastising us than teaching us.

211

Maybe she should start each class with a dodgeball game. That way, the kids can get rid of some that extra energy. If anyone were to ask what the lesson was about, I'd have to say about the need to sit down and shut up when someone is up front speaking. Our teacher said that so much I would have sworn it was in the bible. When class ended, we had 15 minutes to spare before church started.

"Trekela, come with us over to the other building. They're having a bake sale."

Mama gave me four quarters to put in church. I gave $0.50 to the Sunday School offering. The remaining portion would go in the church collection. She didn't give me enough money for the bake sale.

"Okay."

We stood in line behind the other kids.

"No shoving!" the lady behind the counter warned. Remarkably, everyone settled down.

Rashika, Angie and Dara purchased their goodies. I tried sneaking off before the lady behind the counter had a chance to put me on the spot.

"What are you having, dear?"

Too late.

"Um…that's okay. I didn't really want anything."

"It's for the church building fund. When you give to the Lord He won't forget it," she sang.

Do I look like I have money or something? That can't be it with me in this polyester dress with big flowers all over it.

"All my clothes is classy." I should smack Auntie for that comment.

Angie raced to my side and saved me. "Sis. Waters, this is our friend, Trekela. She's a visitor today."

"Ooh, then you get one on the house. Here you go, darling. Enjoy. God bless you!" Sis. Waters handed me the last pink cupcake. Angie winked.

"Ah, man. Why she get one free?"

"Yea. That's not fair."

"Shut up all that whining," Sis. Waters threatened, clapping her hands for added measure. "Quit acting like hoodlums. Show some Christian love to our guest. Now, who's next?" she asked with an unloving, non-Christian-like expression on her face. I could tell she really wanted to cuss, and probably would have if she thought she could get away with it.

"Thanks, Angie."

"Don't sweat it. But next Sunday you won't be a guest. That trick only works once around here."

We went outside for a minute. Kids ran around carefree, messing up their good clothes playing tag. It looked fun. But I didn't want to draw unnecessary attention to myself.

"Trekela!" Ms. Denise walked over to us. "I've been looking for you. Come on. Let's go inside to find a good seat."

Please don't let it be up front, I prayed.

"Ah, Trekela, sit with us," Dara pleaded.

"Unh-unh. Nope, she's sitting with me."

It's nice to be wanted...for once.

Ms. Denise and I found seats in the middle of the center aisle. I preferred to sit in the balcony with Dara and them.

213

Maybe I will next Sunday or the Sunday after that.

I glanced at the program to review the order of service. There's an awful lot of stuff that's planned for this morning. I wonder how long it takes to do everything on the program.

"O God, Our Father...our Redeemer...our Savior...our Lord...God of the heavens...God of the earth...King of kings...Lord of lords...bright morning star..." So began the prayer of the first of five deacons who were on program to pray during the devotion time.

We'll be here for a while.

Towards the end of the third prayer, I realized I hadn't thought about Chester and mama and that whole ordeal since arriving to church.

"...protect our loved ones from all hurt, harm or danger, my Father..."

"Please, Lord," Ms. Denise said as she squeezed my hand. I put my head back down to rejoin the prayer.

I was glad when the preacher got up. The sermon was next to the last item on the program. Plus, I'd hoped he'd slow the Holy Ghost down some. At one point, people from all sides of the building were "caught up in the Spirit" as Ms. Denise called it.

"Don't be scared," she said as she put her arms around me. I looked up towards the balcony and saw Dara, Angie and Rashika not fazed by any of this. So I played it cool, too. I'm glad I didn't sit with them. I'd cried more in this service than I wanted to. Hiding the tears didn't work. Ms. Denise fished out tissues from her purse for me. I couldn't help it. The songs sung by the choir touched me.

As the pastor positioned himself behind the pulpit, things settled down in the audience. Starting off slow, he read from the bible, paying particular attention to how he anunciated each word. He continued in slow, theatrical dialogue, building to a moderate pace, as if he were in a regular conversation, then climaxed to a sing-song, rhythmic pattern, finally ending with the same pace and tone with which he began his sermon.

"While Bro. Peters comes with a selection, the doors of the church are open." He extended his right hand as the five deacons came forward to stand at the front of the church.

> *"Dear friend…God knows what you've been through*
> *that's why He died for you*
> *so remember although your heart is broken in two*
> *that's where you'll find a true friend*
> *who desires a life with you"*

Tears flowed freely as I reflected on the beautiful image of a friend who desired a life with me and was with me, even though my heart was broken.

"Is there one today?…Don't wait another minute…God desires a relationship with you…you don't have to live this life without Him…You can have a new life with Jesus…make a decision to accept Christ and follow Him today…"

I wanted to go up there, but was afraid of all the people looking at me. If only I'd stop crying, I wouldn't be embarrassed in front of them.

"I'll walk with you if you want me to." Ms. Denise must have sensed my desire to receive what the preacher offered - a new life.

I got up. She and I stepped into the aisle, and walked towards the front amid thunderous applause from the audience. However, there seemed to be a concentration of whooping and hollering from one direction. When I got to the front, I looked up. All the kids who sat together in the balcony stood up to cheer me on. Dara clapped with tissue in her hands, while Angie and Rashika tearfully embraced one another. Watching this display by the youth, the adults could not contain themselves. I continued to hold on to Ms. Denise.

The pastor walked up to us. "Is she a candidate for baptism?" he whispered.

"Trekela, why did you want to walk up here?" Ms. Denise asked.

I thought about the pastor's comments during and following the sermon. I reflected back on Ms. Denise's talks at Jesus at the Clubhouse. I tried to find something to say that would tie in with what I'd learned from them. My heart was so full. But nothing eloquent came. So, I settled on three words.

"I want Jesus."

After church, Ms. Denise took me to lunch at Luby's Cafeteria.

"Trekela, I want you to know I love you and I'm committed to being here for you."

"I love you, too."

Grabbing my hand, she added, "You may not feel any different. But trust me, you *are* different."

She was wrong. I knew something changed on the inside of me. I *did* feel different. Peace finally found a permanent place in my heart to call home.

Once we finished eating, she took me to the bookstore to purchase a youth bible. Then she took me home. Turning into the complex driveway we passed RJ, Milton and two girls walking towards Sunnys. Tricky's car was parked in front of the tennis court. Dee Dee stood outside the driver's window, pulling her head out only to laugh. She tried to adjust her shorts in the back, but struggled to get her thumb underneath the material since they were so tight. Her attempts to adjust from the front ran into the same problem.

We pulled alongside the curb in front of my square.

"Here we are."

And here we go.

"I love you, Trekela."

"I love you, too, Ms. Denise." I gave her an awkward sideways hug and kiss on the cheek.

"I'll see you Tuesday at the clubhouse, right?"

"Yes, ma'am."

I watched her drive-off. Afterwards, I faced forward and headed home. Dee Dee's and Tar and Tay's mama sat outside on Dee Dee's porch.

"Hello," I said, out of a good, Christian heart. They looked at me, but said nothing.

I shifted my Sunday School papers and new bible into one hand. "Hi," I said again, this time waving in case Bobby Blue Bland drowned out my voice. They still just sat there.

I continued towards home. Ms. Pat and Darrel were on her porch this time. I caught Ms. Pat pointing at me with her free hand.

"Hi, Ms. Pat. Hi, Darrel."

"Unh-huh," Darrel mumbled, halfway tossing his hand up.

"Hi, Trekela," Ms. Pat said dryly.

As I walked into my apartment, I overheard, "I guess she supposed to be saved now." They both fell out laughing.

That's okay. I'm hopeful brighter days await me.

Author's Afterthoughts

This writing project is intensely personal to me. While not autobiographical, it's still the truth. The struggles outlined in this novel plague the reality of many young girls across this country. Poor choices in friends. Struggles with parents. Being misunderstood. Pre-teen and teen sexuality. Love famine.

When everything in her world fell apart, Trekela looked for guidance in Christ. Her decision didn't reverse all the issues in her life. However, she no longer lived without hope. Hope for the present and hope for the future.

There are only two forces at work with regards to one's life – the force that conspires to destroy life and the one that aspires to enhance it.

The bible teaches in John 10:10, _"the thief does not come except to steal, kill and to destroy. I (Christ) have come that they may have life and that they may have it more abundantly."(NKJV)_

That _they_ is you and me.

Consider the following: *"If you confess with your own mouth that Jesus Christ is your Lord, and believe in your own heart that God has raised him from the dead, you will be saved." (Romans 10:9)*

Do you wanna be saved? Do you wanna make the same decision Trekela made? It's simple. Faith in Christ produces salvation. Anything in addition to that is a mere expression of your beliefs, but not criteria for being right before God. Believe Christ died for your sins. Accept Him as your personal Savior. That's it. You are saved.

Be confident that the One who began this process in your life will also complete it (Phillipians 1:6).

Remember it's not just about going to heaven. God didn't take the time to create you in His image just to see if you could make it to heaven or not. He wants a one on one, intimate relationship with you.

Choose Christ! God bless you.

Lex

Acknowledgments

I thank God for His presence in my heart and life. He truly is a Father who knows how to give good gifts to His children. My wonderful husband, Lewis Rhone, is a nightly reminder to me God always gives His best. I love you, sweetie. Thank you for believing in me.

God also graciously provided me with a host of other family and friends who've been instrumental in seeing this project completed.

To my mother, Emma Means, thank you for your undying love and devotion.

To Kecia Cook, thank you for speaking the words that confirmed this project would come to pass.

To Kimberly Powell, thanks for being "my dawg" for almost 15 years.

To Tra Ki Pullum, thank you for candid input and always making me feel my dreams were attainable, no matter the size.

To Dr. Terrance Woodson, your theological input and genuine support of me will never be forgotten.

To Carroll Scherer, thank you for the timely wisdom that propelled me to pursue my writing dream.

To Monica and Maria Gaston, thank you for assisting me in targeting the proper age group based on "experience-appropriateness".

To my beloved Brittney King, I will never forget the way you passionately interacted with my characters. You are a great encouragement to me.

To Julie Wenah, thank you for reminding me of the need to show the struggles of teens who walk with Christ.

To Candace Johnson, thank you for screening the draft and giving me a sense of how my intended audience will receive the book.

To Evangeline Mitchell, thank you for seeing the possibilities of this project with regards to young women who share our past.

To Renee Porter, thank you for advising me regarding appropriate language for the YA genre.

To Pam Juniel, I wholeheartedly appreciate your feedback as a public school teacher. Thank you for affirming the accuracy of the characters' experiences.

To Lesila Bennett, Rose Leavell and Gailya McElroy, thank you for convincing me of the broader appeal of this project.